Overlap

Overlap

Paul Cockburn

Virgin

With thanks to Danny and Jack Shreeve and the boys of Remove B, plus Mr Ryecroft and Mr Owen, The Mall School, Twickenham, for invaluable market research.

First published in Great Britain in 1996 by
Virgin Books
an imprint of Virgin Publishing Ltd
332 Ladbroke Grove
London W10 5AH

A catalogue record for this book is available from the
British Library.

ISBN 0 7535 0080 9

Typeset by Galleon Typesetting, Ipswich
Printed and bound by
BPC Paperbacks Ltd, Aylesbury

For the real Chris Stephen(s) – heir to the Cockburn millions and future Forest midfielder.

My thanks to Mick Rayner and Mel Hackett of Nottingham Forest FC for their assistance.

Part 1

Part I

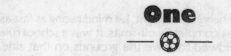

One

Chris had never been inside the old chemical works before. Today, he was breaking all the rules.

He called out at the top of his voice. 'Nicky!!!'

He continued chasing after the fast-running figure ahead of him. Nicky was about 30 metres away, and the gap was growing. Chris had almost caught him at the fence that separated the school from the abandoned factories and warehouses, but Nicky had dropped down the other side before he reached it. After sprinting across the narrow lane, Chris had then stumbled going over the tumbled slabs that had once been the works' wall.

The two bags he carried were slowing him down. He couldn't close the gap, and Nicky wasn't going to stop. Chris was breathing hard, forcing himself to keep going. Every few yards he called out again.

'Nicky!!'

The long open spaces on this side of the old works were ideal for running flat out. Apart from some rusting railway tracks set into the ground and a few cracks where weeds were pushing through, the surface was absolutely flat. Nicky continued to draw away.

In the distance, on a low hill beside the river, was the main bit of the complex, where once-tall chimneys had belched steam and fumes above strange metallic sheds. Most of it had been dismantled when the place closed down – before the school had even been built – but there were a few sheds still standing – big, rusting hangars, open at both ends, with loading bays and vehicle inspection pits, and pipes which they used to use to fill the tankers. Nicky was heading towards the nearest of those.

Chris followed the curve of one of the railway tracks, which eventually swung round the building, running down to the old wharves on the river and the black swing bridge that still sat across it. He cut across to his left, angling more directly towards the shed.

What am I doing here? he thought, his mind racing as fast as his feet. The site was completely off-limits. It was a school rule that no-one was allowed to leave the grounds on that side, though it was a rule which students at Spirebrook had been breaking for ten years. The fence had big holes in it, and the lane was sheltered from prying eyes by some sickly-looking hedges and a few weary old trees.

And if you weren't allowed to venture on to the old lane beyond the fence, it was even worse to consider climbing the high surrounding wall, covered with warning signs. Not that it was much of a barrier — it had fallen down in several places. The contractors who were working in there, off and on — ripping up a bit of the concrete flooring or removing a few more pieces of the dilapidated sheds — were supposed to have rebuilt it, but never would.

Chris knew that if anyone had seen him chase Nicky in here, he'd be in more strife than he had ever seen before.

Still he went on.

Up ahead, Nicky was heading towards one of the old sheds, the one nearest the river. He disappeared through the vast open doorway at one end.

Chris followed the same path, almost stumbling over the steel-lined grooves of yet another set of tracks, worn smooth by the passage of 50 years of locomotives and trucks. He hoped Nicky was heading towards home. It had always been a huge temptation for Nicky to take the short cut along the lane, or even across the old works' site, because his home lay just beyond, on the other side of the main road. For as long as he had known Nicky, though, Chris knew his friend had obeyed the rules. Every morning, Nicky had followed the main road to where it curved round to meet the end of Chris's street. Every morning, they met up in the same place, by a bus shelter near a small shopping plaza.

That was where they had met up that morning. It already seemed a long time ago.

4

Chris ran into the shed, hearing his feet echo off the high walls. Almost immediately, he pulled up, listening for sounds of his friend's progress and scanning the interior of the huge shed for any sign of him.

Nicky had vanished.

'Now what?' muttered Chris, confused and exhausted.

If Nicky was heading for home, he needed to keep going through the shed and out the other end. From there, he could get back on to the lane, and then out on to the main road. From where he was standing, however, Chris could see the whole length of the vast building, and the empty space beyond the far doors. Way off in the distance, there were some JCBs working on flattening the ground at the end of the lane (there was talk that Tesco were going to build a super-store on the old works' site; Chris and Nicky had been holding out for PC World). But no Nicky.

It was dark (and smelly!) inside the huge building, even though the roof was holed in a few places. Looking round in the dim light, Chris saw that there were all kinds of hidden stairways and platforms on both sides. Holding his breath, he listened again for a clue. This time, he heard Nicky's trainers off to the right somewhere; then there was a rusty, grating sound and a loud, metallic bang. Steeling himself to run all the way to Nicky's house if he had to, Chris gripped the bags tightly and set off once more.

Some steps led him up to a high platform and a set of wooden offices against the metal wall. There was a rusted door at the back of one of them.

Chris heaved it open, recognising the same sound he had just heard. He stepped back out into the open air. He had come out right on the river bank. He looked around, feeling his breath hard in his chest. A long stone wharf stretched off in both directions, with large metal bollards spaced along the edge every few metres. To the right, it curved round, wide open ground all the way. Left, then.

More railway tracks embedded in the wharf followed the line of the river, just a few feet from the edge. The water was sluggish and slate-grey. Up ahead, the old swing bridge crossed the river, casting a deep black shadow on the already dark water. The railway's single track ran under it, along the narrow embankment.

There was no sign of Nicky, but he had to have gone under the bridge and on to the partially cleared site beyond, where men in hard hats came twice a year to take measurements for the slowest supermarket building project in history.

Chris called Nicky's name one more time. Although things were getting well beyond a joke, he was determined to sort them out, no matter what.

He plunged into the shadows under the bridge. As he passed into the darkness, from the corner of his eye he glimpsed a shape detaching itself from the deepest shadow, moving quickly towards him. A moment later, something smacked into him, crashing into his body and knocking him sideways to the ground. There was a moment when he knew he was skidding across the wharf, unable to stop, unable to see even where he was going.

He heard a dull splash, as something heavy hit the water.

Everything was going dark. In those few, long seconds, Chris saw the events of the last few weeks replaying through his mind like a dream. It was almost comforting. Perhaps, this time, he would see just where he'd gone wrong . . .

6

TWO

Chris lost his marker as he crossed the halfway line. He angled away to the left, and put on a burst of speed that left the sluggish defender for dead. Chris looked up and saw Nicky fake one way, turn the other, and then race along the right touchline, with the left back trailing behind him.

Cutting back to the right, Chris took off towards the far post as quickly as he could. He arrived just as Nicky's hard, flat cross came whistling over the last defender. The opposition keeper was scrambling across the goalmouth, but Chris knew he just had to keep calm. He took off from his right foot, gliding through the air as if in slow motion, and met the ball with a whip-like crack of his head. He placed the ball back towards the right post, and the keeper never stood a chance. At almost the same moment as he landed, Chris saw the ball hit the back of the net.

There was a distant yell or two as the small group of spectators celebrated. They sounded almost as relieved as they were happy. Chris wheeled away behind the stranded keeper and ran towards Nicky. They high-fived and banged heads.

'Nice header,' said Nicky, grinning. 'I thought for a moment you weren't going to keep up.'

Chris laughed as they turned towards their team mates. 'You'll never be fast enough to out-run me, Nicky . . . I thought I was going to have to wait for ever for the cross to arrive!'

They both laughed, knowing that they were too well matched for either to ever beat the other by much. They ran back towards their own half and the congratulations of their team mates.

Chris glanced at the sideline. Mr Lea, the sports teacher,

gave him the thumbs-up. Three-nil and only ten minutes left. Blackmoor, their arch rivals, were beaten.

Chris drew in a deep breath and waited for the kick-off. The last few minutes of the game passed quickly, and the final whistle signalled the start of Spirebrook's celebrations. One of the Blackmoor players stretched out his hand towards Chris. 'Good game,' he said, his voice showing his disappointment.

'You were unlucky,' Chris replied. Next moment, he heard a joyous shout, and turned to see Nicky running across towards him.

'That wasn't so tough!' he grinned, slapping Chris on the shoulder.

The Blackmoor guy extended his hand. 'Good game,' he said again.

Nicky's eyes flashed. 'You were useless,' he responded.

They stood face to face. The Blackmoor player's fists were clenched and his face contorted angrily. Chris nudged his friend from behind.

'Don't be such a prat, Nicky . . . they gave us a good game until half-time.'

Nicky laughed and turned away. Chris paused for a moment, watching as the guy from Blackmoor stared at Nicky's back. Then he followed his team mate towards the dressing rooms.

Chris half-expected the Blackmoor team to be lined up outside the dressing room as they left, but there was no-one around. Mr Lea hurried them on to the bus. Chris fell into the seat beside Nicky. 'It wouldn't hurt you to shake a few hands at the end of a game,' he said.

Nicky gave him a disbelieving look. 'They're just losers, Chris – why bother?' Chris wondered if he should try to explain what he meant, but his mate was already changing the subject. 'Semi-finals next, then! Wonder who we'll get?'

Thursdays started with double geography, but that didn't sour Chris's mood as he walked to school the following morning. All the night before, and from the moment he had woken up, he had felt stupidly pleased with himself.

The win over Blackmoor had been a good one. Chris replayed the third goal in his mind. Even though he and Nicky

8

had combined that way dozens of times, it still felt special whenever it clicked. Chris had known exactly where the ball was going to fall. It was like magic.

Chris heard a shout and looked up. Nicky was at the bus stop – Chris would have recognised him from a mile away. He also recognised the black jackets worn by the boys clustered around Nicky. Black for Blackmoor.

'Hey!' yelled Chris, breaking into a run. He closed the distance between himself and the others quickly, dropping his bag to the pavement as he arrived. The Blackmoor lads turned to face him, although one still gripped Nicky by his shirt. Chris recognised one of the others as the guy Nicky had refused to shake hands with. Several of the others were older – and bigger. 'What's going on?' he shouted.

A big, ginger-haired Blackmoor thug snarled back at him. 'Why? You want some?'

Chris felt his heart beating faster. There were eight of them.

The kid from the Blackmoor football team pushed to the front until he was face to face with Chris. 'Stay out of this,' he warned.

Chris saw that Nicky was still firmly in the grip of a hard-faced guy, maybe two or three years older and six inches taller. 'It's OK, Chris,' he called, struggling wildly. 'I'll deal with it!'

The boy holding him slapped him across the back of the head. 'Yeah? You and whose army?'

'Hey!' Nicky yelled back. 'I'm Italian. I've got eight brothers and two sisters . . . and even my sisters could take you on!'

The hard-faced guy slammed Nicky against the bus shelter. Chris stepped forward but he felt helpless – the odds were stupid! He tried to think of a smart way out of the situation. The ginger-haired kid was grinning at him, like he was daring Chris to try something.

Inspiration hit Chris like a lightning bolt. 'Nicky! Go round the full back!' Chris knew it sounded dumb, but he knew Nicky would understand. Just like magic. Of course, if he didn't, then Chris was about to find himself in big trouble.

The ginger-haired guy was staring at Chris like he was mad. 'This isn't a game of football, stupid!' he snarled.

'Just as well,' replied Chris, his heart in his mouth, 'because everyone knows how useless Blackmoor are at football.'

Ginger-head's face twisted with rage, then he lunged at Chris with his fist. Chris ducked but the blow still clipped the back of his head. He felt the Blackmoor bully reach out to grab him, and stuck out his foot. The ginger-haired kid went over Chris's shin and fell to the floor like a sack of potatoes.

Two or three of the others were reaching out for him, and the others had all turned to look his way. Nicky took his chance. He stamped on the tall boy's instep and barged him in the chest. The boy went over his own school bag and landed on his back.

The Blackmoor gang were clearly caught in two minds, unsure if they should be chasing Chris or Nicky. They still had Nicky penned in, and two of them stepped forward, trying to make sure he stayed that way. Nicky, though, was in space, and he knew how to use it. Just as he had out-foxed the Blackmoor full back all through yesterday's game, he faked as if he was going one way, then weaved the other.

The two Blackmoor boys were left grasping at thin air. The others, their mouths wide open with surprise as Nicky burst through them, didn't even move. Only the football player seemed to react, and he was closer to Chris. His hand snaked out and grabbed at Chris's jacket. Chris felt a moment of panic – if he didn't get away in the next few seconds, the others would be able to get him too. With all his strength, Chris pulled away, feeling his jacket tear as the sleeve came loose. He lashed out with his free hand and chopped his assailant on the wrist. In that moment, the guy from Blackmoor lost his grip, and Chris turned away. He and Nicky fled towards the precinct as fast as they could run.

There was an old cafe on the corner, a place where mini-cab drivers and shoppers stopped for lunch and endless cups of tea. Before school, though, it was always full of Spirebrook sixth-formers. Chris and Nicky burst through the door just a few steps ahead of the chasing Blackmoor pack. The black-jacketed gang froze in the doorway. Now it was their turn to be outnumbered. There was a long moment of silence, then they slowly turned away.

Chris was breathing fast, and he sank into one of the vacant chairs. It took him a moment to remember that he had left his bag by the bus stop, but there was no way he was going back to get it just yet! Nicky, meanwhile, had walked to the door. As the Blackmoor lads backed away, he started to chant.

'Four-nil, four-nil, four-nil, four-nil . . .'

Three

Spirebrook Comprehensive was a grey monstrosity of a
place, with three main buildings and a sports hall. It was a
dump, tucked away on the outskirts of the sprawling city of
Oldcester, pinned between a main road and a dirty old river.
Spirebrook had once been a small market town, but it had
been swallowed up by the growing city years before. The
comp had been built in the sixties: four ugly concrete slabs
near the river on an old railway yard. Its one saving grace was
that it had a long, curving playing field. Along the widest part
of the field, between two electricity pylons which stood like
metal giants at either side, lay the school football pitch.

On their first day at the school, Nicky and Chris had had a
bet over who could kick a ball over the electricity wires first.
Nicky had won.

Mr Lea was out on the pitch, picking up litter, as Nicky and
Chris walked under the covered way that led to the middle-
school building. 'We've got Oakby in the semi-final!' he called.
'They beat Eastbury five-two. Tell the others, will you? And
don't forget training Tuesday!'

'Sad!' exclaimed Nicky. 'Five-two! Mind you, Eastbury are
rubbish ... Remember when we played them a couple of
years ago, Chris?'

Chris remembered. Eastbury was a big school in a town
about twenty miles away. They had played Spirebrook Under-
13s in the third round of the County Schools Cup two years
before, and had beaten the 'Brooks 2—0. Chris had been
marked out of the game by a huge kid with black hair.
Obviously Nicky didn't remember the game in the same way.

'Where is Oakby?' Nicky asked, screwing his eyes up as if he
was trying to look at a distant map.

'Near Salisborough,' Chris replied.

Nicky looked back over his shoulder towards the football pitch. 'Flea didn't say if we're home or away.'

Finding out would have to wait. Mr Lea had disappeared. Besides, they were almost late for class after their run-in with the lads from Blackmoor, and Chris was already going to have a tricky job explaining why his school bag was missing (they'd spent twenty minutes searching for it, but with no luck; Nicky's bag was just where he had dropped it, inside the bus shelter).

Chris took another look at the ripped shoulder of his jacket. Two teachers had commented on it already, and his father was going to throw a fit. Nicky didn't have a mark on him, for all the roughing around their opponents had given him. Typical. Nicky had all the luck in the world sometimes.

'What was all that about you being Italian?' Chris asked.

Nicky grinned, his eyes bright with amusement. He loved putting one over on other kids. 'Had them going, didn't it?'

'Not really,' answered Chris. 'Just because you have an Italian surname, doesn't make you a member of the Mafia, you know. Even your dad has never been closer to Italy than Margate.'

'My grandad was born there!' Nicky insisted. 'Or was it my great-grandad?'

They passed through the doors into the middle-school building. Chris continued ragging his friend. 'And you haven't got eight brothers, you've got one. And he's only three years old!' They were both laughing now.

'I was right about my sisters, though!' Nicky replied. 'Either of them could have taken that lot! What a bunch of losers!'

'Just try not to upset the whole Oakby team as well, OK?'

Nicky shrugged. 'Don't even know where Oakby is,' he complained.

'It's south of here.' Chris sighed.

'Anywhere near Margate?' Nicky asked.

They continued like that all the way along the corridor.

As far as Chris was concerned, it didn't matter where Oakby was. The game could have been in Italy, Africa or even on

Mars and it would have been all the same to him. Chris just liked to play; anytime, anywhere. Ever since his dad had first taken him to watch Oldcester United play when he was five, Chris had been hooked on football.

It had been a magical game. Oldcester were in the old Third Division, before there was a Premier League, and they'd drawn Coventry City at home in the third round of the FA Cup.

Two-nil down at half-time, United had come back to level the game, thanks to a scorching free kick from the edge of the box by Bobby Foster and a scrambled goal in the last five minutes. Chris's dad had gone hoarse with cheering, and Chris had talked about nothing else for a month. All that winter, he had practised taking free kicks out in the back garden.

It hadn't mattered that they lost the replay 4–1, or that Bobby Foster had been sold to Everton later that year for £950,000. Chris carried the memory of that game inside him.

Chris loved watching football, but over the years he had also discovered that he loved playing even more. He had played for his primary school, and when he went up to Spirebrook, he had been a natural choice for their team too. Chris was tall for his age, with long legs and natural pace. He was strong too, and could shake off tackles. He was good in the air and could use both feet on the ground, though it was his fierce right-footed shot that served him best. He had also learned how to curve the ball in the air.

He had teamed up with Nicky because of football. Nicky Fiorentini came from a family of football players. His uncle had had three seasons with Juventus in the 1960s, and two of his cousins played for a good non-League side down near London. Short, dark and hot-tempered, Nicky was a naturally gifted player, capable of making the ball do tricks other players could only marvel at. He could curl a pass 50 yards round a defender, and had great balance and vision. With Nicky in midfield and Chris up front, Spirebrook had found a partnership that could do no wrong.

That year, Chris had scored eighteen goals in ten League games, and had been a major factor in their wonderful run in the County Schools Cup. All they had to do now was to get past Oakby, and they'd be in the final, which was played at Oldcester's ground! There'd be hundreds of spectators! Well, a few dozen, at least. Certainly more than they'd ever had before!

Even though the game was a month away – and there was the small matter of Oakby to be dealt with first – Chris felt a small twinge in the pit of his stomach every time he thought about the possibility of stepping out on to Star Park and playing in that final. Star Park – Oldcester's home turf. If they got to the final, Chris would play on the same pitch as his heroes, in the same stadium he visited twenty times a season to support United. Nothing, but nothing, could get in the way of that happening.

Ms Robinson, the geography teacher, was collecting in homework that morning. Chris had finished his after the match. Football – practice and matches – took up a lot of his time, but Chris's father always made sure he kept on top of his school work. Today, of course, his homework was safely in his school bag – wherever that was.

He explained as best he could, but he knew Ms Robinson didn't believe him. He promised to do the work again. Ms Robinson continued to collect the papers. 'Nicky Fiorentini,' she called, looking into the centre of the class. 'I don't seem to have your homework either.'

Chris looked round. Nicky sat close by on his left. He was wearing a big, stupid grin. 'It's not finished, Miss,' he replied.

Chris groaned.

'Mum and Dad were working late and –'

Ms Robinson wasn't interested. 'Was there a football match last night, Nicky?' When Nicky nodded, Ms Robinson's face clouded. 'We've talked about this before, Nicky. Football can't interfere with school work. I said I'd speak to Mr Lea if you continued to avoid doing your homework. Is that what you want?'

Nicky looked flushed with anger. Chris reached out and tapped his arm. Nicky flicked a glance at Chris and seemed to calm down a fraction in that second. He sighed. 'No, Miss,' he replied at last.

'I want the work handed in tomorrow, Nicky. Four hundred words on the countries of Latin America.'

Nicky jolted upright, stung by the words. 'Four hundred, Miss? I thought it was only three hundred.'

'At least you can count, Nicky,' Ms Robinson snapped sarcastically. 'Think of the extra hundred words as a bonus for winning last night.' Then she added, 'Chris, I hope you're not starting to get into the same bad habits as your friend. Make sure I get your homework too.'

Nicky sat sullenly through the whole lesson. As they left the classroom, he pushed a smaller lad out of the way.

'Take it easy,' said Chris.

Nicky turned. 'She can't do anything. She wouldn't dare tell Flea to take me off the team. And if she did, he wouldn't listen. Not with us so close to the final. It's the biggest thing that's happened to this school in thirty years! There's no way that Flea will let himself be forced into dropping me!'

'I wouldn't count on it,' Chris answered, quietly. He was feeling pretty sore about getting into trouble about the homework. 'Why not just get the work done? I'll lend you a hand, if you like, seeing as I've got to do it again.'

Nicky laughed. 'Not with your grades, Chris! I'll ask Jimmy Guest. He owes me a favour. If you're going to cheat, at least get decent marks for it!'

They set off to their next class. By the time they reached the science block, Nicky was in a much better mood. 'Geography! What's the point in it anyway? Tell me one useful thing we're going to learn in geography.'

'How to find the way to Oakby?' Chris offered. Nicky swatted him with his bag.

Four

A week or so later, Chris and Nicky arrived at after-school training to find a heated discussion going on in the dressing room.

'What's going on?' Nicky demanded, barging through the crowd. Chris followed him through. At the centre of the scrum, they found Pete Baynham, the team keeper, sitting on one of the benches, looking very hot and moody and the centre of some loud, excited questioning. 'What's happening?' Nicky demanded again, louder than anyone. He was face to face with Griff, the team captain. Griff was a year older and liked to think he was in charge. As always, Nicky got his own way.

'Pete can't play in the semi-final,' Griff explained.

Chris felt his spirits sink. Pete was a good keeper but he didn't get the jersey because he was some kind of superstar. There just wasn't anybody else.

Nicky had turned on Baynham. 'What's the matter with you?' he yelled. 'You injured or something?'

The other boy dropped his head. He was on the brink of tears, twisting his gloves between his fingers. Griff finished detailing the problem.

'His dad's got to go to Bosnia. His mum's decided she doesn't want them to live on the Beckford estate while he's not there, so they're going to live with some aunt or something.' Nicky looked up and glared at Griff as if he still couldn't see the point. 'In Hartlepool,' Griff explained.

'So what?' stormed Nicky. 'He can come back for the game, can't he? Or they could leave after the semi-final. It's only a week away!'

'It's a bit far to come back for a day,' sighed Chris, a little

17

tired of providing Nicky with geography lessons.

'Mum says we're leaving on Sunday no matter what,' muttered Baynham. 'There's been all kinds of rows, but she won't change her mind.'

Chris pressed through the last few of the boys clustered around Baynham and sat on the bench beside him. 'Maybe Mr Lea could have a word,' he offered. He didn't hold out much hope. He'd met Mrs Baynham before, and he doubted that Mr Lea would want to be on the same planet as her if she was in a mood. 'When does your dad go?' he asked.

'Saturday,' replied Baynham.

Chris stood up again. 'Come on, guys, there's nothing we can do about it now. We'd better get changed and out on the field before Flea thinks he's lost the whole team.'

The others gradually stepped away, still arguing over what was to be done. Chris put his jacket on the peg beside Baynham's and started to get changed. Pete was already in his kit, but he sat there quietly for a few minutes until he saw the others start to file outside. Chris and Nicky watched him go.

'Must be quite rough, having a dad in the army,' Chris commented. 'They're always moving around. I suppose his mum gets a bit fed up.'

Nicky screwed his face up to show that he wasn't that bothered with the problems of the Baynham household. 'We need him in goal,' he insisted.

Chris thought about the situation as he laced up his boots. After Pete Baynham, Spirebrook had very few options in goal. 'Maybe we ought to go and see his mum. See if there's anything we could do.'

'Like what?' scoffed Nicky.

'She might let him stay with one of us –'

'Brilliant!' cried Nicky. 'He could stay at your place.'

'Why my place? Your house is loads bigger.'

'Yeah, and it's always full of aunts and cousins and babies and old ladies. There's hardly room in it to swing a cat.' They trooped out on to the school field, past the ugly pylon that hovered over their heads. 'Bosnia . . . that's where they're having all the trouble, right? In Yugoslavia. That's near Italy, you know.' Chris was impressed. He clapped his arm across

18

Nicky's shoulders and grinned warmly. Nicky still looked very thoughtful. 'So where's Hartlepool, then?' he asked.

It wasn't a happy practice session. Pete Baynham was miserable and flopped around between the posts like a sack of potatoes, and the rest of the team were just as half-hearted. Nicky hardly broke into a run for an hour, but just shouted at the others when passes went astray.

Once the session was brought to an early halt by a burst of heavy rain, Mr Lea told them all to get changed and then see him in the gym. The rain was drumming on the roof of the gym as the boys pulled off their kits and headed for the showers.

'I have two bits of news for you,' Mr Lea announced, once they were all settled on the floor in a half-circle. 'First, the team for tomorrow night's League game will be unchanged from last week's, except that Mike Hurst will cover for Steve until he's got over the flu.' A few mutters floated up from the boys; they had all expected that change, and most thought it wouldn't affect the team at all badly. Steve managed to get ill so often, it was more of a shock when he was actually playing. 'As for next week's Cup game – well, as you know, Pete won't be available in goal. So, I'm going to give the shirt to Donald MacIntyre.'

Chris sighed, and heard Nicky join in the chorus of disapproval. No-one was happy with that decision – least of all Donald, who Chris saw was sitting off to one side with a frightened expression on his face. Donald was a small lad, several inches shorter than Baynham. He was quick, and brave to the point of being stupid, but he didn't have Pete's experience.

But what other choice was there? A few stupid names were offered – two of them by Nicky – but Donald was the best of a very short list. They'd be left critically short of height at the back.

'All right, all right,' Mr Lea shouted, trying to quell the angry complaints. 'That's enough. We'll do some work at defending from corners and free kicks next week and bring him up to speed.'

'Speed isn't the problem,' commented Nicky sourly. 'A pair of stilts is what we need.'

'Thank you, Fiorentini. Let it drop for now.'

'Oakby will slaughter us! It's hardly worth us turning up!'

Chris nudged Nicky in the ribs. He never knew when to shut up!

'Well, now, it would be a pity if you didn't, because someone is going to be at the game to see you. That's the second bit of news I have to tell you. His name is Raymond Foulds, and he's a scout for several clubs in the Premiership and Endsleigh League, including Oldcester, Leeds and Manchester United. He always comes along to the semi-finals of the County Cup to see if there are any promising players he can sign up. I'm told Oldcester still have places in their School of Excellence for next season. It's a great chance to show what you can do.'

Chris felt his heart-rate pick up. A talent scout! A chance to get a trial with Oldcester! Suddenly, the big match had become even more important. They had to do well!

Everyone was talking at once. Mr Lea tried to quieten them down so that he could make himself heard.

'Only the best will even get asked to attend a trial, but one or two of you might be in with a chance.' Nicky's face split in a wide grin. 'What matters most, though, is the game. We deserve to be in the final. If you can pull together as a team, you'll make it.'

The meeting was over. The boys rushed out from the gym, anxious to carry the news home. Only Chris and Pete Baynham were left behind. 'Don't feel bad, Pete,' Chris told him. 'You'll get another chance at your new school.'

Pete shook his head slowly. Chris knew there was nothing he could say to make it any better for him, and that it would be best to leave the keeper on his own. He left quietly, to find Nicky pacing around in the playground like he was a big cat waiting for dinner to pass by. The rain had eased off.

'Come on!' Nicky called. 'I want to get back and tell my dad. He's going to be on the phone all night once he knows. I expect we'll have a crowd of ten thousand there to watch us by the time he's finished!'

'Listen, you go on without me,' said Chris.

Nicky's face passed from excitement to puzzlement. 'What are you up to?' he asked. Chris wasn't sure. The idea that had popped into his head earlier was still swirling around in there.

'I'm just going to wait for Pete — make sure he's OK,' he told Nicky.

'Oh. Right.' Nicky hesitated for a micro-second. 'I'm off then. See you tomorrow.'

Just as Chris had expected, there was no way Nicky would want to be around someone as miserable as Pete Baynham. By the time Chris had turned back towards the door, Nicky was splashing through the puddles, halfway to the school gates.

Chris was late home and his father wasn't in a good mood. Dinner was almost ruined. Chris fetched his plate from under the grill and wolfed the food down quickly, ignoring the burnt bits and the lumpy gravy, while telling his dad that it tasted fine.

They watched the last ten minutes of *Deep Space Nine* in silence, then Chris carried the plates into the kitchen. They washed up in silence. Chris had plenty of time to wonder if his bright idea was as clever as he hoped.

'You got any homework tonight?'

'Half an hour's maths,' Chris replied.

His dad nodded. 'Come in here a minute. I need to talk to you.'

They went back into the living room and his dad turned off the TV. Chris sat on the couch while his father settled into his favourite chair, fidgeting with his remote control and picking imaginary fluff off his trousers. Chris waited. It sounded like more bad news was on the way.

'The boss came to see me today,' Chris's father began. 'Things are going to be a bit quiet over the next month, so there isn't going to be much overtime. We're going to have to be a bit careful.'

'Right,' replied Chris.

'I'll have to let Mrs Shaw go,' his dad continued. 'That means we'll have to do all the cleaning ourselves.'

21

'Right,' said Chris again.

'And, I'm afraid –' His dad looked up and Chris waited for the axe to fall '– we'll have to miss the rest of the away games this season.'

Phew! Was that all? Chris waited to see if his father was going to add anything else. Nothing came.

'I understand,' he said, feeling greatly relieved. Chris's dad looked relieved too. He was slowly letting a smile back on to his face. 'We're still going to the home games, though, right?'

'That's what season tickets are for, Chris.'

'Great. No problem. I don't even mind if I don't get much of a birthday present this year.'

Chris's father eyed him suspiciously. 'It shouldn't come to that,' he replied. 'Unless I have to keep buying new school jackets.'

'That won't happen again,' said Chris insistently.

'Fine.' They both sat in their seats, letting the tension unwind. Finally, Chris's father stood up. 'I suppose you want to watch *Top of the Pops*,' he said. 'I'll just go and get a few jobs done while –'

'Wait!' called Chris. 'Don't you want to hear my news now?'

His father sat back down. 'Am I going to like this news?' he asked.

'Most of it,' said Chris.

Saturday. The centre of Oldcester was jumping with people shopping. Chris, his father and Nicky picked their way through the crowds. They saw Pete Baynham with his mum and dad, waiting outside Burger King. Pete was wearing a bright white shirt and his face was split with a huge grin.

'You must be Peter,' Chris's father said as they came to a halt. He gave the boy a long look over, then turned to give Chris a quick glance. Chris was looking very pleased with himself. His father then straightened and offered his hand to Mr Baynham. 'I'm John Stephens,' he said.

Mr Baynham took his hand in his own big grip and shook it. 'I'm Gareth and this is Trish,' he said, indicating Pete's mum.

'I'm Chris and this is Nicky,' said Chris, offering to shake hands with Pete. The boys all laughed.

'This is really good of you, you know,' said Mr Baynham. He had a strong Yorkshire accent and he looked about twice the width of Chris's dad. 'Pete was really upset about the game, but Trish couldn't stay in that flat while I wasn't there. We get burglaries and all sorts on the estate.'

'I understand. He's welcome to stay with us for a few weeks.'

'I couldn't believe it when I heard you'd agreed he could stay with you until after this semi-final,' added Mrs Baynham. 'It means a lot to Peter.'

'I'm sure we'll get on fine.'

'I was worried about leaving him on his own, what with his dad going overseas, but Chris persuaded me that Peter playing in the semi-final would be the best for everyone.'

'Yes, he's very persuasive,' Chris's father agreed. Chris wasn't sure he liked the way everyone turned to look at him at that moment. He tried hard to avoid looking back at the adults. So far, no-one had worked out that he'd told Mrs Baynham it would be OK if Pete stayed at his house *before* he'd checked it out with his father.

'And are you sure about this afternoon?' asked Mr Baynham.

'It'll be fine. We borrowed a season ticket from a friend who can't make it. Chris organised that as well.'

Mr Baynham looked at his watch. 'We'd best be going, then. I only have a couple of hours before my ride comes, and I'm still not packed. Trish will drop off Peter's things at your house tomorrow, OK? She's catching the eleven-thirty train.'

'We'll be ready.'

The Baynhams said their goodbyes. Mr Baynham gave Peter such a fierce hug that Chris wondered if he might miss the semi-final through injury anyway. Finally, they separated, and Chris's father led the three boys back across the market square.

By the time they reached the main road, they were in the middle of a steady stream of people making their way towards the river and the smart new stadium that sat on its banks, gleaming in the hot sun. All around them, people were converging on Star Park, clad in replica shirts, scarves and hats; some with their faces painted, others with their hair streaked in red and blue. There was a buzz of excitement in the air. The crowds grew thicker and noisier. Someone let off an air horn.

Baynham jumped. Chris and Nicky both took a long look at Pete's shirt, and then exchanged one of their telepathic glances. Both removed their scarves and wound them around Baynham's neck.

'What's all this?' he yelled.

'You can't come in here wearing that shirt,' Nicky explained. 'We've got standards to keep up.'

'This game is called football,' continued Chris. 'It's not the same game you lot play up there . . . it's got skill and everything.'

'We beat you in the Coca-Cola Cup!' protested Baynham, now swamped in blue and red. A complete stranger came over and dumped an Oldcester hat on his curly red hair.

'A lucky penalty,' Chris explained. 'And we hit the bar twice! Now, shut up and we'll try and explain the game to you before it kicks off . . .'

Five

'Remember what we talked about,' said Mr Lea. 'Quick passes. Use the wings. Their defenders are big lads, so don't hit high balls towards the middle expecting Chris to win them all. At the back, I want tight marking and I want strong tackling. Get involved. Concentrate. Especially you, Fiorentini.'

Nicky spun round to face the front. 'Yes, sir.'

Mr Lea tossed an orange at him, which Nicky caught. Chris finished lacing his boots and tucked his blue shirt into his shorts. As always, he rubbed his hand on the badge for luck.

Mr Lea stepped back. 'Go and show them what we're made of,' he said, and as each of the eleven ran past him on to the pitch, he high-fived them. Chris was last in the line; another of his superstitions. 'Make it happen, Stephens,' Flea whispered as he ran past. Chris followed Nicky out into the middle.

Nicky was running backwards. Chris turned to see what he was looking at. Over on the sidelines, there were about 30 people who looked like they'd won a Nicky lookalike contest; all with the same short bodies, black hair and white teeth bared in big grins.

'Which one is your cousin?' asked Chris.

'What cousin do you mean?' Nicky asked in return.

'Exactly.'

Nicky didn't get it. His eyebrows twisted down in a deep frown and his lips curled in the corners. 'Which one do you think he is?'

Now it was Chris's turn to be puzzled. He followed Nicky's searching glare along the touchline. He had no idea what he was looking for.

'Who?'

25

'The scout! The talent scout! Frank Doo-dah!'

'Ray Foulds.'

'Yeah, him.'

'How should I know? Come on Nicky, concentrate!'

They finished the warm-up routine and watched as Griff lost the toss. Oakby decided to have the wind at their back in the second half. The ref tossed the ball to Chris and he walked into the centre circle to start the game.

He risked one last look along the sidelines, to see if he could figure out which of the spectators might be the elusive scout. The Fiorentini clan leapt up and down in their long coats, waving frantically and shouting '*Forza* Spirebrook!' as if they were watching AC Milan play Inter.

Chris grinned to himself and got ready for the whistle. Scout or no scout, there was a game to be won. He reminded himself of what was at stake – a final match at Star Park, and the County Schools Cup.

'Make it happen,' he whispered. Then the whistle sounded, and the game was underway.

❂

It was a disaster. Actually, things had started brilliantly – five minutes in, Nicky had caught Oakby's keeper off the line and chipped him from fifteen yards. From then on, the game had been going steadily away from Spirebrook, though.

Oakby had a big centre back with razor-cut hair, who stuck to Chris like glue. The few times he'd been able to lose him, Chris had been picked up by the sweeper. The two occasions he'd beaten him too, he'd been fouled. He hadn't had a sniff of a goal.

After that brilliant start, Nicky drifted out wide and played little part in the game. The midfield players had been over-whelmed, and Oakby had started flooding against the Spire-brook defence like waves hitting a sea wall.

Just before half-time, things had taken a turn for the worse. Oakby's striker had collided with Pete Baynham, and they'd both ended up with gashed heads. After all Chris's hard work, they'd ended up with Donald MacIntyre between the sticks after all.

To make things worse, after the collision the ball had trickled into the empty net. They were all square at half-time, and the wind would be pushing up behind Oakby for the next 45 minutes. Flea had gone off to the doctor with Baynham, and Griff had been left to sort out the mess. Spirebrook's big day was turning into a farce.

The second period saw Oakby pour forward. The exhausted Spirebrook defence buckled, and they could have gone down 5 or even 6–1. MacIntyre, though, played out of his skin and saved everything they threw at him until, at last, he and Micky Hurst hesitated as a high cross came over, watching each other instead of the ball, and one of the Oakby strikers headed the ball into the net.

Chris set the ball down and made ready to restart. To his amazement, he found Nicky bounding over to stand beside him.

'You see that?' asked Nicky, looking off to the side. Chris turned to try and see what Nicky had spotted. 'That guy, getting out of the car. I bet that's him! I bet that's Foulds! He's been sitting in his car all along.'

Chris turned back, heavy-hearted. 'Then he's come to watch us get beat,' he snapped.

Nicky shook his head. 'No, he hasn't,' he said, with a glint in his eye.

They kicked off. Nicky took the ball and ran at the Oakby defence. He beat two defenders but the last one robbed him. 'Come on, Spirebrook!' he yelled. 'Push up in support! We can get this back!'

Nicky went wide, picked up a pass and took on the full back. This time he won a corner. Before anyone had a chance to think, Nicky played it short and took a return pass from Sean Dolan. He slipped round two defenders and whipped a looping shot a foot over the bar from 25 yards.

'What's got into him?' asked Griff on the way back.

Chris could have answered, but he preferred to keep his thoughts to himself. Nicky's sudden change of mood had brought a new pace to the game, and Oakby were struggling.

Over the next five minutes, the game changed character completely. Nicky had the legs of the full back, and started to make one dazzling, mazy run along the right wing after another. With the pressure off, the Spirebrook midfield were

27

able to press forward, and as he felt support coming up behind him, Chris saw some space at last.

Time, though, was running short. Chris knew they'd have to score quickly, or Oakby would just shut up shop and run off the rest of the clock.

Nicky was in possession again. The full back lunged in, prepared to bring Nicky down in order to stop him, but his clumsy sliding tackle found nothing but air as Nicky danced away, the ball at his feet. Another Oakby player was nut-megged. Nicky was in the clear. All he had to do was make his way to the goal-line, and Chris could get on the end of one of his telling crosses.

To his amazement, Chris watched Nicky cut inside, aiming for the angle of the penalty area. The sweeper went over and Chris peeled away from the razor-cut defender marking him, heading for the far post. As the keeper went off his line to narrow Nicky's view of goal, Chris found himself completely unmarked and facing an open net.

'NICKY!' he yelled, and he saw his team mate look up and take in the situation with a single glance. In that split second, Chris expected the ball to arrive, and clearly so did everyone else. The keeper hesitated and the sweeper tried to move into the space.

But Nicky didn't make the pass. Instead, he took the ball wider on the outside of his boot, away from the sweeper. Now there was only the keeper to beat, but the angle was getting very tight. The goalie started to spread himself as Nicky drew back his right foot to strike.

The shot hit the keeper's body and went under him. The pace had been killed but the ball was spinning wildly, curving towards the goal.

Chris and the sweeper realised at the same moment that the ball was running along the line between them. Chris reacted a fraction quicker, racing in to tap the ball over the line.

The shout from the touchline was as loud as anything Chris had ever heard outside of a professional game. He jumped high into the air, punching at the sky with his fists. As he landed, he looked for Nicky. His partner was on the floor, not having moved after he hit the shot.

'You OK?' Chris called.

Nicky didn't answer. Instead, he glared at Chris, pulling himself slowly to his feet. Chris didn't have time to figure it out – Griff and the others had arrived to bury him under their celebration.

Six edgy minutes later, the ref blew for full-time. Chris walked back to the centre circle, elated at having saved the game, but troubled by Nicky's reaction. When he got there, Nicky was sitting near Fuller, head bowed. Chris left him to it. Everyone had their own way of preparing for one of these shoot-outs – they were such nerve-wracking ordeals, and worse than any other part of the game.

Chris sat by Fuller and Griff, who were on Flea's list to take penalties as well. Griff was looking very calm.

'That goal's knocked the stuffing out of them,' he whispered to Chris. 'Look at them, they're really down!'

Chris took a glance around at a few of the nearer Oakby players. They did seem more tired than Spirebrook's, and a few of them were looking quite pale at the prospect of the shoot-out.

'We've got them . . .' Chris muttered to himself.

Penalty shoot-outs are played as much in the mind as they are on the pitch, and when Chris stepped up to take Spirebrook's first kick, Oakby had already missed their first. Chris made up his mind to drill the ball into the bottom left corner, and the Oakby goalkeeper didn't even move as the ball flashed past him.

Sean scored his, then the third Oakby player spooned his kick over the bar. Fuller swaggered up to the spot and blasted his down the middle. The Oakby keeper got his hand to the ball, but was almost carried into the net by the force of the strike.

At 3–1, all Spirebrook needed was to get one more, and Griff marched forward to take his kick. None of the Oakby players could watch; their heads were down, their fatigue and misery draining the last ounce of hope from them. In contrast, although a couple of Spirebrook players turned their backs, the rest were watching joyfully as Griff placed his kick to the keeper's right.

It was all over. They were going to the final!

29

The whole Spirebrook team leapt to their feet to embrace Griff, and were then mobbed in turn by their supporters – mostly mums and dads and substitutes. They had enough Fiorentinis to go round three times.

'Where's Nicky?' Chris asked when he surfaced from a long hug from grandma Fiorentini. The old lady shrugged, and then started shouting extremely loudly in Italian. Chris remembered she was stone deaf.

'Here,' came the reply.

Chris turned, expecting to see his closest friend grinning. Instead, Nicky had a face like a wet weekend, all thunderstorms and black clouds.

'What's the matter with you?' Chris asked.

'That was my goal,' Nicky hissed.

Chris looked quickly to either side. So far, no-one had noticed their confrontation amidst all the jubilation. 'What do you mean?'

'You stole that goal to make yourself look good,' Nicky said icily.

Chris laughed. What an unbelievable thing to say. Surely Nicky was joking? He had to be!

'If you hadn't jumped in, it would have been my goal,' Nicky continued.

'Nicky . . . the sweeper would have cleared it off the line. Besides, what difference does it make? It was our goal! It saved the game!'

'It was my goal,' said Nicky. 'It was my game.' Next moment he was swept away from Chris by jubilant relatives. For a moment, Chris was left alone in the middle of the celebration. His mouth hung open and his arms were limp at his sides. Something had just happened, but he didn't know what. Suddenly, he couldn't remember why he had been so keen to win this game.

Six

'Hi. Chris Stephens, isn't it? My name is Ray Foulds. Do you have a minute? I want to talk to you about a few things.' Showered and changed, Chris was sitting on the step at the back of Spirebrook's mini-bus. He was trying to figure out what had happened to Nicky; what had made his best friend act the way he did. This should have been a day to celebrate. Instead, Chris felt miserable. 'I take it Mr Lea told you I was coming?'

'He's not here,' Chris commented. 'He's taken our goalie to get his cut looked at.'

'I saw.' Foulds nodded sympathetically. There was a short silence. 'Congratulations, by the way,' Foulds said suddenly.

Chris checked him out. He looked about 50, with short hair, going a little thin and grey. He had a strong face and warm brown eyes. His suit looked a bit worn but his shirt and tie were brand new. The tie had the Oldcester club badge on it.

'Thanks,' Chris replied, looking back at the ground.

'You were lucky,' Foulds continued. 'They had the best of the game for an hour. It's only my opinion, mind, but I think they're the better team.'

Chris looked up. 'Then why did we win?'

'Because you had the better players.'

Chris almost laughed. He was starting to get the idea that Foulds wasn't all there.

Foulds must have seen the uncertainty on Chris's face. 'Just because you've got great players, it doesn't always mean you've got a great team. Sometimes, the rest of the side can't live up to the standards the best players set. Then there are times when . . . well, let's just say that good players don't play well together.'

31

'Which are we?'

'I'm not sure. It's easy to see why Oakby are so good; they play well as a unit. They support each other, work hard. They have a good understanding. There are no outstanding players among them, but they manage to look as if they've got fifteen good players on the pitch.' Chris recalled what it had felt like when Oakby had taken control of the match. No matter where he'd run, there never seemed to be any space. If he looked up to play a pass, every blue Spirebrook shirt seemed to be marked by two in Oakby green. 'Still, you won on the day, and that's what counts. And I think there are two or three of you with a real future in the game. Look, I shouldn't be speaking to you, not without Mr Lea being here. Could you give him a message for me?' Chris nodded. 'I'll call at the school on Tuesday. I'd like to have a chat with three of you about attending a trial at Oldcester later this month.'

At last Chris looked up, and there was the beginning of a new look of pride and pleasure on his face.

'Who?'

Foulds grinned. 'You, Fiorentini, and the keeper . . . what's his name?'

'Baynham.'

'Isn't he the one that got hurt? I meant the other lad. Danny, is it?'

'Donald,' Chris replied. 'Donald MacIntyre.'

'Scottish, is he?'

'Sort of.'

'A decent Scottish goalkeeper. I should probably call the Scottish manager – he might want him for the Europeans.'

They both laughed. Chris could feel the gloom lifting from him like mist. He had completely misjudged Foulds: the Oldcester scout was all right.

'We've always thought Pete was better –'

'Nah, too big. He's good in the air, but too slow getting down. That's why he got hurt, I reckon. He's probably right for you in the short term, but Donald's your man, especially if he can just grow another few inches. It happens, sometimes. A shorter boy just keeps on growing, and winds up bigger than his mates.'

'His dad's a midget,' Chris informed Foulds.

'Oh well.' Foulds sighed. 'We'll have a look at him anyway. For Scotland's sake.' They both laughed again. Foulds leant forward and clapped Chris on the shoulder. 'I'll see you Tuesday,' he said, then turned away and headed back to his L-reg Mondeo. Chris watched as it crept out of the car park and turned towards the city centre.

Almost before Foulds had disappeared, Nicky appeared in front of Chris as if he had sprung out of the ground.

'Happy now, thief?' he snarled, his eyes blazing with anger and his fists clenched. Chris pushed himself to his feet as Nicky stepped even closer, almost pinning Chris to the back of the bus.

'What's your problem, Nicky?'

'What? You think I didn't see you?' Nicky yelled, grabbing at Chris's jacket. 'You steal my goal, make yourself look a big hero, and then you're all pally with the scout guy. Offer you a contract, did he?'

'No!' insisted Chris. He was as confused by Nicky's attitude as before, but he was also starting to get pretty stiffed with his friend's accusation. He pushed Nicky's hands away from his collar and tried to get past. Nicky kept grabbing at him, shouting angrily.

'You've always been jealous! I'm the better player and you know it!'

Chris could feel his anger and disappointment boiling over. He pushed, and watched as Nicky stumbled and fell back. He heard something rip and then Nicky hit the floor hard. Chris stood over him, his fists clenched tight.

'You're not better than me, you're not even half that good,' he roared. 'But just so you know, Foulds wants to see both of us on Tuesday. He didn't care who scored the goal, he didn't even care who won today. If things work out OK next week, we might get a trial at Oldcester. That's it; that's all we talked about, OK?'

He was breathing hard by the time he finished. Nicky kept very still, looking back up with a strange expression on his face. Chris stepped past him and went off to find the rest of the guys, so that they could get back in the bus and go home. He didn't want to be in the same place as Nicky for even a moment longer; he didn't even want to have to think about him.

It was an hour later that he realised that the top pocket on his jacket was torn. He thought about what his dad had said and groaned.

Seven

Chris had a pretty miserable weekend – there was no home match to go to, Pete Baynham was miserable because they were supposed to go to Nicky's house to play on his Play-Station, and Chris's dad was furious over the jacket. In fact, things got so bad that Chris camped in the bedroom all day Saturday, grinding out a massive amount of homework. Feeling a little better, he went downstairs at 4.40 to see the vidi-printer announce that Oldcester had gone down 2–1 at Spurs, thanks to a late Sheringham winner.

'To think we nearly signed him,' sighed his father.

'Yeah, if we'd just had another two million quid to spend,' Chris said bitterly.

On Monday, Nicky didn't turn up at school. The angry concern that had been nagging at Chris had to wait another day. He wanted to get this business sorted out. He and Nicky had been friends too long to fall out over which one of them had scored a stupid goal!

So it was with some relief that Chris saw Nicky waiting in the usual place on Tuesday morning. He ran over to the bus stop, leaving Baynham trailing behind; almost laughing when he realised Nicky was waving at him.

'Where were you all weekend?' Nicky asked.

'What do you mean?'

'I thought you were coming over?'

Chris opened his mouth to reply, but realised he hadn't got a clue how he was going to explain what he had been thinking.

'We were kind of busy,' he managed at last.

Baynham caught up and the three of them turned to begin the journey along the main road.

'Where were you yesterday?' Baynham asked.

Nicky's face lit up in a broad grin. Chris knew at once that he had some secret. With Nicky, that meant the conversation would go all round the houses before it came out.

'Can't say. Family business.'

'Mafia wedding?' asked Chris.

'Something like that. Did you see *Match of the Day* on Saturday?' The others said that they had. 'What about that Sheringham goal?'

'It was pretty good,' admitted Chris.

'Good? Didn't you think it was a mile offside?'

'Alan Hansen said —'

'Oh, what does he know, Pete? He's from Liverpool.'

'They did all right on Saturday, didn't they?'

'Yeah, yeah,' said Nicky abruptly, obviously keen to move on from Liverpool's performance. 'You see the Manchester game yesterday?'

Chris noticed the excitement in his friend's voice. 'Sure. Good win.'

'They were awesome. Giggs made those other saps look like they were a hundred years old. And what about Cantona's goal, eh? He knew it was going in the top corner from the second he hit it. He just turned away —' Nicky mimicked the Frenchman's wheeling run, one hand raised in salute '— and ran back to the halfway line. He *knew* it was going in.'

'We won on Saturday,' announced Baynham, scratching at the large plaster on the side of his brow. Chris winced, remembering how bad the wound had looked at first. In the end, Flea had taken Pete to hospital for a couple of stitches. His mum had been *furious* when they called her on the phone. She'd almost come to get him there and then.

Nicky frowned, his memories interrupted.

'If you didn't have Yeboah, you'd be fighting relegation. Leeds aren't in United's class.'

Chris was about to ask if Nicky meant Oldcester or Manchester United, when Nicky stopped and pointed across the street towards a row of lock-ups. His face was bright with amazement.

'Chris — look! Isn't that your bag?'

And it was, up on the roof. They ran over the road and,

climbing up on a shopping trolley they found overturned behind the garages, Chris got up on the roof and recovered his bag.

'Nothing missing!' he exclaimed. 'Look – here's that stupid geography homework I had to do again!'

'As soon as I woke up this morning, I knew today was going to be special,' said Nicky, beaming. 'I just knew it.'

The day dragged towards its end. Chris and Nicky raced from their last class as if they were coming out of starters' blocks. As they walked round the back of the science block, Nicky spotted a metallic blue L-reg Mondeo in the teachers' car park. With a loud cheer, they raced each other over the last 50 metres, slamming into the gym doors together.

They found Ray Foulds and Mr Lea in the gym, drinking tea from Flea's thermos. The scout was talking about a couple of lads he'd seen two or three years ago, at a club in Leicester which had a youth team. The two boys – both centre backs – had played a major part in making this team into one of the strongest in the area. Opposing strikers had come to hate playing against them. Then one had gone to Forest's youth team, and the other had had a trial with Coventry. Almost at once, both had gone off the boil. Now neither was going to make the grade – they were a brilliant pair, but neither of them was quite good enough on his own.

Flea nodded at the boys to come over. Donald MacIntyre was sitting on a bench, pale faced. The PE teacher listened as Foulds finished his tale, then added a thought of his own.

'I remember when Cottee and MacAvennie were together at West Ham,' he said. 'Best year the Hammers ever had. Third in the First Division. Sold them both afterwards, but they never managed anything like as well on their own. We ended up signing them both back after a few years! Trouble was, they came back at different times. I reckon, if they'd stayed with us in the first place, we could have won the Championship.'

'Never mind, sir,' said Nicky, in his most false polite voice. 'I expect you'll get a chance to win the First Division next year.'

Chris stifled a laugh. He caught Foulds covering his mouth with his hands too.

37

'We're not relegated yet Fiorentini,' Flea responded. 'You'll see.'

He finished his tea and placed the two cups back on the thermos. Then he clapped his hands together like he was running a training session.

'Right, you know why you're here. Mr Foulds saw you play against Oakby and he wants to talk to you about it. I'm sorry we didn't sort it out last week, but I was ages at the hospital with Baynham.'

'Maybe the bang on the head will do him good,' muttered Nicky, to no-one in particular.

Flea indicated that Mr Foulds should take over. Chris was bursting with excitement, even though he knew roughly what was coming. The scout made to stand up, but suddenly Nicky butted in.

'Excuse me, sir. Can we wait for my uncle?'

Everyone turned to look at Nicky. Chris stared at his friend, wondering what was going on. Nicky hadn't said anything about this.

'Your uncle, Fiorentini?'

'Yes, sir.'

'This is just an informal chat, son,' said Foulds. 'I shall be coming to talk to all of your parents soon.'

'I know,' said Nicky, 'but my uncle said he wanted to hear what you were going to tell us today. He said he'd be here before quarter to. Is it all right if we wait?'

Foulds and Flea exchanged glances. The scout shrugged. Flea looked a little angrily at Nicky, and then agreed they could hang on for a while. Having said that, he started looking at his watch every 30 seconds as if he was in a desperate hurry to be somewhere else.

Foulds settled back, resting his back against the wall bars. They waited in silence for a few minutes.

'I was talking with Mr Lea about your partnership before you came,' the scout said, catching Chris by surprise. He'd been looking out of the window, waiting for Nicky's uncle to appear. 'You've had a productive year or two together.'

'Yes,' said Chris. Nicky also shrugged his agreement.

'I've heard a few reports on how you two work together. You tee them up, and you knock them in, right?' His eyes flicked from Nicky to Chris as he described their partnership.

The boys answered simultaneously.

'That's right,' said Chris.

'Not always,' said Nicky, scowling.

'No,' said Foulds, keeping his eyes on Nicky. 'Actually, I saw the goal you got on Thursday.'

'Which one?'

If Foulds had any idea of the dangerous ice he was walking on, he didn't show it.

'The chip, at the beginning of the game. Nice touch.' Nicky beamed widely, although Chris noticed his friend was twisting his fingers through the handle of his school bag. 'The game almost went away from you though. You kept them in it, I thought,' he said, with a smile at Donald.

'We won, though,' said Nicky.

'You drew. I've never liked these penalty shoot-outs, although I suppose you have to have them these days.'

'And the second goal?' asked Nicky. Chris looked across, hoping that Nicky wasn't about to make a fuss again. His friend, though, looked quite calm and happy.

'Not bad. It was a bit risky, trying to take the ball wide. Wouldn't it have been better to have crossed the ball to Chris earlier?' Nicky's jaw dropped. Chris didn't know whether to laugh or cry. Foulds thought it was a *cross*? 'Still,' said the scout, 'it ended up in the back of the net. That's the main thing, eh? Oh – is this your uncle?'

It was, and Nicky just about managed to close his mouth again by the time his Uncle Fabian clattered through the doorway, trying to remove his shoes before he walked on the courts.

'I'm sorry if I've held you up,' he said. 'Please, start now. I don't want to interrupt – I'm just here to listen.'

He sat down on the bench, on the other side of Donald. The bench almost tipped up. Fabian Fiorentini was a large man.

They all slid up a foot and settled down again. Flea was staring up at the ceiling. Finally, everyone was as comfortable as they were going to get, at which point Mr Foulds stood up and moved so he was in front of them. He looked at the three boys seated along the bench, rubbing his chin with one hand. Having thought about what he was going to say, he spoke.

'I spoke briefly with Chris last Thursday, so I expect you know who I am.' Everyone mumbled their agreement, including Uncle Fabian. 'My name is Ray Foulds,' he continued, which made Chris wonder why he'd bothered with the sentence before. 'I played centre half for Oldcester in the sixties. Since I retired from the game, I've done a bit of coaching, and I was youth team manager for a while, but now I just do a bit of scouting; looking for new players for the youth squad.

'I'd heard Spirebrook had two or three decent players from different people, so I wanted to see for myself. Now, last week might not have been your best performance of the season, but I still think Oldcester might want to take a look at you three. So I've spoken to the club and they'd like you to come along to a sort of open day next Saturday, after the home match with Blackburn, and then attend a trial session at the training ground on the London Road on Sunday. What do you think?'

'Brilliant!' exclaimed Chris. Donald gave a nervous nod. Nicky didn't say anything, Chris noted, but looked quickly across to his uncle.

'If things go well, the club might want to talk to you about joining the youth squad and attending their coaching school, but that's in the future. First, the trial, and then we'll take it from there, OK?'

Chris nodded, his excitement almost boiling over inside him. He turned to share it with Nicky, but his friend was still looking along the bench. Uncle Fabian was raising his hand.

'Yes?' asked Foulds.

'Excuse me asking, but do you only scout for Oldcester?'

Foulds narrowed his eyes, wondering where this was leading. 'Not just them, no.'

'Only Nicky . . . well, he might not want to get too close to just one club right away. He might want to keep his options open, in case something better comes along.'

Chris couldn't believe what he was hearing. What could be better than a trial with Oldcester? He didn't have long to wait to find out. Uncle Fabian was trying to be diplomatic, but Nicky was too impatient.

'I heard you also scout for Manchester United.'

Foulds nodded his head. He was obviously starting to see what was going on. 'That's sort of true, yes. I don't have a formal tie with them, but I recommend players to them, sometimes. However, because I work with Oldcester, I have to give them first —'

'Would you recommend me?' Nicky interrupted.

'Is that what you want, Nicky?' Nicky gave a casual shrug, but Chris could tell from his eyes that Nicky knew exactly what he wanted. 'I could send them a report, maybe. See if they're interested.'

'They're interested,' said Nicky, ignoring a warning hiss from his uncle. Chris listened carefully, knowing that Nicky was about to reveal the secret he'd been storing inside all day. 'We spoke to someone yesterday, an agent. He says Manchester United would want to take a look at me. He says they'd pay ten thousand to sign —'

The room fell silent for a long few seconds. Nicky had halted, having seen Foulds suddenly becoming very angry.

'They wouldn't do that,' he said, in a low voice.

'But this guy said —'

'I don't know who this *agent* is,' Foulds continued, raising his voice to cut Nicky off, 'but he's wrong. It's illegal to offer players under sixteen or their families any kind of financial inducement. Manchester United wouldn't break the rules. Nor would any other club I'd introduce you to.'

Uncle Fabian had risen to his feet very quickly, coming round to stand behind Nicky. He rested his hands on his nephew's shoulders. Nicky took the hint and shut up.

'Please, don't misunderstand. Nicky is just over-excited. We spoke to this agent; he spoke to some people at Old Trafford. They'd like to see us. They said you could arrange it. This isn't about money; we just feel Nicky would do better at a bigger club.'

Foulds rubbed his chin, taking a moment to think.

'I'll make a few calls. But this doesn't change anything I've said. No money changes hands over young players, not if I'm involved. And I want Nicky to come to the trial at Oldcester on Sunday.'

'Of course, we'll be there. Thank you.' Uncle Fabian offered his hand and Foulds shook it, though he still looked pretty unhappy. The Fiorentinis stood up. Uncle Fabian waved goodbye and Nicky winked at Chris.

Moments later, they were gone. Chris watched through the window as they crossed the playground. He thought he could hear them arguing.

'Well, I think we'll leave things there for now,' said Foulds, pulling on his coat, 'unless either of you have any questions.' The two remaining boys shook their heads. Actually, Chris had several thousand questions that needed answering, but he doubted Mr Foulds would be able to help. 'Come to the ground early on Saturday, say, one o'clock. Go to the office. They'll have some special badges for you and your parents, to get you into the ground. And there'll be a spot of tea after the game, and a chance to have a good nose round, OK?' This time they both nodded. Foulds gave them both a warm smile. 'Saturday, then.'

He shook hands with Flea, and they both headed for the door. Chris and Donald MacIntyre trailed after them. Donald looked as if he was in shock. Chris left him and went to find Pete Baynham, who was waiting for him near the gate.

'Good news?' asked Baynham.

'I'm not sure . . .' said Chris quietly.

Eight

He didn't become any more sure over the week that followed. He and Nicky had one short conversation about the meeting with Foulds one lunchtime. It was difficult for Chris to talk freely because Baynham, Griff, Fuller and a few of the others were listening. The trial had become the hottest topic of conversation in the school.

'You're going to play for Manchester United?' scoffed Fuller, scruffing his hand through Nicky's hair.

'Get off!' snapped Nicky.

'You sure it wasn't Manchester City?' asked Griff. 'The way they're playing you might get a game with them.'

'You'd be lucky to play for Stoke City,' replied Nicky, trying to switch attention away from himself. It didn't work.

'Manchester United aren't going to want you,' Griff counterattacked, making sure he got right into Nicky's face. 'They've already got too many foreign players. They'd want somebody English.'

'Or someone who could play football,' sneered Fuller.

'You'll see, soon enough. At least I'm going to get a trial there, which is more than you'll ever do, Fuller!'

Several of the others jeered, and then a few left-over bits of lunch flew back and forth. Fuller's temper was a match for Nicky's and there was a moment when Chris thought a fight might break out, but then Fuller caught sight of someone who owed him money and he scooted off across the playground in pursuit.

'Is that true, Nicky?' asked Chris. 'Have you got a trial sorted out with United?'

'Could be . . .' Nicky replied evasively.

'So what about Oldcester? You going to the trial there?'

'Yeah!' Nicky insisted. 'Can't do any harm, can it?'

Chris gave it a moment's thought. 'So who's this bloke you've been speaking to, this agent? Did he really say he could get you ten thousand quid?'

Griff whistled. Chris could see that their team captain was about to start telling them what he'd spend the money on, so Chris cut him off by throwing the crust off somebody's sandwich at him.

'So? What did he say?'

Nicky leaned a little closer so that only Chris could hear. 'He said he knew people at Old Trafford, and that they're always looking for good youth players.'

'And what about the money?'

'You know how it is. There are always ways of doing things like that, so that no-one knows. Managers bend the rules all the time. Look at what happened to George Graham.'

'He got caught.'

'That's not the point. All I'm saying is this agent reckons there's money there, if it'll help things along. He reckons the game's full of people who say they play by the rules, but who do anything they can to make sure they come out on top.'

Nicky was looking unbearably pleased with himself. Chris looked him over carefully. It was like Nicky had changed, somehow, over just the last couple of weeks. It was as if something had been ignited in Nicky's soul. Chris wasn't sure he recognised him any more.

'I always thought we'd carry on together,' he said, feeling a little sad. 'You know, in the same team.'

'Well, why not?' asked Nicky. 'Why don't you have a word with Foulds? He could fix it so we both went up to Old Trafford. He'd listen to you. Come on – it'd be brilliant if we both got stuck in up there!'

'I don't know . . .' said Chris, resting his head against the wall.

He'd never considered playing for any other team than Oldcester. It had been a dream since that first game, with Bobby Foster wearing the No. 9 shirt; the shirt Chris had wanted to fill ever since.

'Go on. At least have a look! Don't tell me you'd say no to ten thousand quid.'

'Who's got ten thousand quid?' said Fuller, returning to the group. Griff pointed at Nicky. 'Lend us 50p then,' Fuller wheedled. 'Parker still hasn't paid me back my money, and I'm dying for some crisps.'

Things didn't become much clearer after the visit to Star Park on Saturday. Nicky arrived with two-thirds of the Fiorentini clan, who seemed most put out to discover that there were only four passes for them, and that the match was otherwise all-ticket. When Chris arrived with his father and Baynham, twelve Fiorentinis were still in the office, complaining bitterly. Seeing as four tickets had been put back for Chris's group, that left one spare, but passing that on to Nicky's mum only seemed to cause a fresh row, with everyone trying to convince her that they were the most worthy recipient. Mrs Fiorentini seemed to be the only person not interested in it.

'First crowd trouble at Star Park for years,' Chris muttered, 'and it's Nicky's cousins who'll have caused it.'

Going inside got them away from the mayhem in the office, at least. There were drinks in an executive suite, and then they went down to special seats in the directors' area to watch the game. Nicky was sitting at the far end of the row, flanked by his father and Uncle Fabian. One of his cousins arrived a few minutes later to take the fourth seat.

The four of them made as much noise as the rest of the crowd in the first half, when Oldcester and Blackburn were evenly matched and there were goal chances at both ends. Come the second half, though, Shearer and Sutton got two apiece and Barry Pacey was sent off for a second bookable foul. As the match ended, someone in the crowd with a radio announced that both West Ham and Southampton had won, which left Oldcester looking a little too close to the relegation zone for comfort.

'You've got Leeds mid-week,' said Baynham, trying to make them feel even more depressed.

'Well, that's three points to us then,' replied Chris, though his heart wasn't in the challenge.

After the game, they were given a tour of the ground. They

even got to meet a few of the players, including Oldcester's Dutch midfield star, Piet van Brost.

'I hear you're coming for a trial tomorrow,' the Dutchman said. 'I'll see you there, perhaps.'

'You're going to be at the trial?'

'Maybe. A couple of the other guys too. Should be fun, yeah?'

Chris wondered if Nicky had been told the news yet. He looked around but couldn't see any of the Fiorentinis.

They caught up with them when the club chairman took them to see the trophy room in the new Easter Road Stand. A central glass cabinet displayed mementos of Oldcester's greatest triumph, an FA Cup win in the fifties. There were other trophies, commemorating divisional championships, a single appearance in the UEFA Cup, the Autoglass Trophy from three years before, and some other stuff. Chris lingered longest in front of a display showing the medals won by the youth team over the last five years. From bright, colour photographs, the faces of boys not much older than him smiled back with their hands on cups and shields and vases — eight trophies in all.

Just along from there, there was a picture of Bobby Foster knocking in the winner against Portsmouth in a game that had won them the old Second Division title. Chris smiled. He could remember the game as if it were yesterday. The city of Oldcester had thrown a party that had lasted three days.

'Chris! Come and see this!' Nicky was parked in front of another case of old photos, from the 1960s. Chris went over. 'Look! It's Ray Foulds! See? Look at all that hair!'

Chris grinned. Foulds must have been the first hippy in the League.

'Where were you just now?'

Nicky chuckled. 'I've been talking to Alan Shearer! Uncle Fabian talked our way into some room upstairs where they entertain the away team.'

'Don't tell me, Shearer said you could go for a trial at Blackburn!'

Nicky frowned. 'Don't knock it, Chris. I mean, would you want to play for this lot if you could play for one of the bigger clubs? Just look around. One FA Cup in a hundred and ten years! Never higher than seventh in the Championship. And after today, you'd have to say that it's starting to look as if they're going down.'

'Is that why you're not wearing your shirt today?'

Nicky giggled. 'That was Uncle Fabian's idea. Said we mustn't look too keen or turn off any of the bigger clubs.' Uncle Fabian was talking to a smart young man in a pale suit. He waved Nicky over to join him. 'I'd better go. See you tomorrow?'

'How are you getting there? Only my dad's working –'

'We'll pick you up!' said Nicky. 'No worries. Get plenty of sleep tonight, Chris – we've got to look our best tomorrow!'

Nicky ran off. Chris turned back to the photo of a hairy, young Ray Foulds. He was just about to nutmeg a Liverpool defender. The caption said he'd scored a hat-trick as United had beaten the Reds 4–1.

'And we still could,' Chris whispered to himself, before crossing the room to find his father.

Nicky arrived early. He was in his cousin's ratty old Chevy, a classic car he was supposed to be fixing up, but which looked more a candidate for recycling each time Chris saw it.

They parked up near the training ground and were passed through the gate. Chris and Nicky both gaped as they saw how many boys were there already. Early though they were, there were already 40 other boys in kit, warming up in front of the changing rooms.

Ray Foulds spotted them and went over.

'Well done, I'm glad you're here early. I just wanted a word.'

'Are all this lot here for the trial?'

'Not all of them, no. The youth team are practising here today.'

'So how many kids are we up against?' asked Nicky.

'You're not against anyone. This is just a chance for the club to see what talent there is out in the schools. About twenty-five boys have been selected.'

'Bloody hell,' muttered Nicky.

Foulds shot him a look. 'Donald is here already. Come on,

get changed and warmed up. You've got a lot of work to do.'

Foulds wasn't kidding. The trial proved tougher than anything they'd ever done in school training. Even the warm-up session was tougher than some of their training evenings. They spent twenty minutes stretching and loosening up, then the coaches ran them round the pitch a couple of times before splitting them into teams. The goalkeepers went off on their own, but each of the main groups went round six stations over the next two hours, with a different exercise and a different coach at each station.

Finally, they took a break. Chris went to find Nicky, and discovered him lying flat on the grass, looking more dead than alive.

'My toenails hurt,' he wailed.

Chris laughed. 'How'd you get on?'

Nicky sat up. 'OK.' He shrugged. 'That coach with the blond hair kept saying I didn't work hard enough.'

'I think he said it to everyone,' agreed Chris.

'Did you see how close they put the cones together on the dribbling test?' Nicky pointed across to where twelve cones were placed in a short line. 'Flea never puts them that close together. I think we should tell him that's how we ought to do it from now on.'

'I take it you did OK on that test,' said Chris.

'Of course,' Nicky replied, in a way that showed he didn't understand why Chris should have asked. 'Did you see what happened when they let my cousin have a try?'

Chris had. Having played a bit of non-League football, Nicky's cousin had tried to talk 'shop' with the United coaching staff, who had agreed to let him take a run through the drill.

'I think he was hoping he'd look so good they'd sign him,' said Nicky.

'Shame he tripped over the first cone!' replied Chris.

They shared a long laugh over that, then finished draining their drinks bottles. The coaches were splitting the group into five-a-side teams.

'We'll play across the pitch, twenty minutes each way,' said the blond coach. 'Each trial group will go up against five members of the Oldcester youth squad. Let's see what you can do.'

48

Chris and Nicky were paired together in the third game to start. As they met their team mates and filed on to the field, Nicky grabbed Chris's arm.

'Look – see who that is?'

Chris followed Nicky's outstretched arm. Lining up with the opposition was a player they'd last seen in the black shirt of Blackmoor Comprehensive. Or, to be more precise, the absolute last time they had seen him, he had been wearing a Blackmoor school uniform, surrounded by his mates at the bus stop.

'*He* plays for the youth team?'

'This could get interesting,' Chris said, grinning. He lined up opposite the Blackmoor player.

'Well, well, look who it is!' The other lad grinned.

'Small world,' said Chris.

'Small pitch,' the other boy replied, with a hard glint in his eyes. 'You won't be able to run away so easily this time.'

Less than a minute after the kick-off, Chris found out what he meant. He took a pass from Nicky on his chest, looked for room to turn, and hit the ground hard as the Blackmoor guy clattered him from behind. Chris picked himself up, aware that he'd taken a whack around the ankles. From several yards away, the boy grinned at him as if to warn him that wasn't the last bruise he'd get.

It wasn't, and Nicky was on the receiving end of a jarring tackle as well. Their team went 2–0 behind.

Chris felt his determination start to burn. He wasn't going to be made to look bad by some chimp from Blackmoor who'd sooner settle grudges than play football.

'Nicky! This way!' he called, angling a run across the defender. Nicky released the ball at once.

Out of the corner of his eye, Chris saw the boy from Blackmoor closing in, stretching to take Chris at the moment the ball arrived. Letting the ball run, Chris hurdled the clumsy challenge, leaving the defender sliding along on his backside, then sprinted after the ball. He dragged it back with his heel and lifted it with his instep as he stepped in towards the goal. The shot was still rising as it hit the net just under the bar.

In the second half, Nicky laid on a perfect pass for Chris to tuck in a second goal, but they still lost 5–2. The best thing to be said for their performance was that they didn't get hurt.

'That was tough!' puffed Nicky as they limped off the field. Chris nodded his agreement. The youth team players were mostly older than them, and it was hard work getting past them. It was even harder tackling the opposition while they had the ball. Nicky had tried twice, and largely given it up as a lost cause.

They broke for lunch. Chris and Nicky found MacIntyre, and quizzed him about his morning.

'I've never been so tired!' he moaned.

'Hah! Goalkeepers have it easy,' scoffed Nicky.

'Not today, they don't. I've faced about a hundred corners and another hundred free kicks. They had six guys in a row, and as I saved a shot from one, the next one would hit the ball. I had to dive, get up, dive again; first one side, then the other.'

'It's a hard life,' Chris laughed. Donald had clearly had a great time, even if he did look a bit shell-shocked.

'Then Piet van Brost came over, and took half a dozen penalties against me.'

Chris and Nicky were all ears now.

'How many did you save?' asked Nicky.

'I never got near one of them,' sighed Donald. They all laughed. 'Lastly, I played a five-a-side, and we lost six-one. I don't think much of my chances.'

'We lost five-two,' said Chris, to show their luck hadn't been much better.

Just before they were due to restart, Ray Foulds came over with a younger man in an Oldcester track suit, who he introduced as Sean Priest, United's youth development officer.

'You guys are at Spirebrook Comp, right?' asked Priest, and they told him that was right. 'How are you enjoying our little test?'

'Great!' said Chris. Nicky was beaming a wide smile and trying to make it look as if he was finding it easy.

'Well, you're doing OK. I'd like to make a suggestion, if I may. Well, two suggestions, really. First, you're not getting stuck in enough, especially you.' He gestured at Nicky. 'That's leaving your team short of possession. Now, I know it's hard, because your opponents are bigger, so what I'd suggest is that you play a little closer together when you're not in possession; support each other against the man on the ball. Then, if you get possession, you should lay the ball back, and then try to move into space quickly. I like the way you two work together when you come forward. Any questions?'

'What about Donald?' asked Chris.

Foulds smiled and crouched down so that he could put his arm round MacIntyre's shoulder.

'Mac and I have had a chat already. He knows he doesn't have the height to play at this level, but we're going to keep in touch, and if he can just grow a bit bigger, we're going to have him playing for Scotland in the World Cup. Right, Mac?'

Donald laughed. Chris had never heard him called 'Mac' before; suddenly it suited him.

'You're going to stay with us today though, aren't you, Mac?' asked Priest. 'Play in another couple of games?'

'Piet van Brost said I could face a few more penalties,' Donald – Mac – reminded him. He turned to Chris. 'I'm going to stop one if it kills me.'

'Good man,' said Priest. 'Right, you two, you're first up this afternoon. Look lively, and remember what I said.'

Immediately after lunch, there was another five-a-side session like the one before, only this time the coaches kept stopping the game to point out different things, mostly about finding space and thinking ahead. One coach urged Chris to shoot on sight more often. Chris listened, and found himself feeling more and more confident, even against the bigger players they faced. He tried his best to remember what Priest had said, tackling back whenever they lost the ball. It was a painful experience.

Nicky was having an even better time. His tackling wasn't any better, but he was starting to play his natural game, full of free running with the ball at his feet. He set Chris up twice and scored two himself. By the end of the game, he was dancing round defenders at will, feinting one way then the other, stepping over the ball and then turning the defender inside-out, or showing off with big, extravagant passes across the pitch.

51

They came off exhausted, but 4–3 winners. They stretched out on the side of the field, trying to catch their breath.

'That felt . . . brilliant!' gasped Nicky.

'It was just like he said . . . we'll have to try . . . defending like that . . . at school.'

'It means a lot more running around,' wheezed Nicky.

'Tell me about it.'

The coaches went over a few more points while everyone recovered their breath, then split the trialists into two teams, the Blues and the Reds. Mac reappeared just in time to be selected as the Reds' keeper. He was beaming all over his face.

'I stopped two,' he said, grinning and rubbing his wrist.

Chris grinned back. Nicky laughed as he replied, 'They'll be the last shots you do stop – we're playing for the Blues.'

The last session of the day was a 30 minute each way ten-a-side on the all-weather pitch. All the trialists were pretty tired, but Priest and the coaches urged them to make one last effort.

It was a draining game, with the ball running quickly on the hard carpet pitch. First-touch control was vital, and passing had to be extremely accurate. An older boy was playing alongside Chris up front, which gave him some help when the Reds had possession. Nicky was pulled back to a central position just in front of the back four. Chris knew he would hate it.

Sure enough, Nicky soon started drifting wide. The Reds went 2–0 up. Just before half-time, Nicky ran wide on the right, took a pass, and flicked it over into the middle. Just like always, Chris knew exactly where Nicky was going to place the ball, but he was tightly marked and couldn't get a sight of goal. Taking the ball on his chest, he laid the ball back to the other striker, who blasted it home past Mac's despairing dive.

As they took on some fluids at the break, the coaches went over to talk to them again. Sean Priest made a beeline for Nicky.

'I told you to stay back. I don't want you drifting wide.'

'Hey! We just scored a goal because I went outside!'

'And you let in two because the Reds are being given too much time in midfield. Your job is to shut them down and to hurry them out of possession. When you get the ball, don't try to run at them; spread the ball around to these two, or play it behind the defence.' Nicky scowled, the way he always did when he was made to do something he didn't like. Priest turned to Chris. 'Nice lay-off. You judged the ball very well.'

Chris started to say that he always knew where Nicky was going to put the ball, but Priest had already turned away to talk to someone else.

Nicky walked out on to the pitch for the second half in a moody silence. Chris could feel trouble brewing.

The Blues couldn't make much happen in the second half, and Mac had fifteen minutes of trouble-free rest. Nicky stayed rooted in the centre of the field, and when he did get the ball he hit hopeful passes over the defence that skipped over the pitch much faster than Chris could hope to run.

'Come on, Nicky, you can hit the target better than that,' Chris urged him. The coaches were saying the same thing, only more forcefully.

Nicky glared at the touchline. 'I'm in the wrong position,' he muttered.

Finally, though, things got a little better. Nicky threaded one pass through that the other striker managed to reach, and they won a corner. Chris headed the cross just wide.

Suddenly, the coaches were urging Nicky to get forward. He set off on one run, but was brought down. Chris saw how tired his friend looked as he pulled himself up.

A couple of minutes later, Nicky attacked again, and this time he beat the centre back and stormed up the middle. For a change, it was Chris who was playing wider. He was completely unmarked, but Nicky had his head down and was dribbling towards the goal, with one last defender retreating in front of him. He feinted both ways, then slipped past him, bearing down on Mac in the Reds' goal.

Chris followed him into the box, running in from wide, but he was sure that Nicky wouldn't need his help. He only had the keeper to beat. Drawing back his right foot, Nicky set himself to level the match.

Then, just as he started to swing through with his right foot, Nicky's left slipped on the carpet. It wasn't much, but it threw him off balance. The shot came off his toe, moving to Mac's left, and with very little force behind it. Nicky howled with pain as he saw Mac throw himself to the side and parry the shot. He buried his head in his hands – he couldn't believe what had happened.

It wasn't over yet, though. Chris raced after the rebound and pulled it in from the goal-line with the outside of his boot, turning to face the goal. Two defenders had raced back towards the line, and Mac was pulling himself up, but if Nicky had been watching for a pass, Chris knew a goal would have been a formality.

Chris took the only other option open to him, even though the angle was incredibly narrow. He drew his left foot across the ball and bent a high, looping shot towards the far post. It sailed over Mac's head and clipped the woodwork as it came down just under the bar, dropping into the net.

'YES!' yelled Chris, and he heard his team mates cheer as they came up to congratulate him. It was one of the best goals Chris had ever scored. He couldn't imagine a better day to have done it on.

Nicky was still sitting in the middle of the goal. He was clutching his ankle. His face looked very red and his eyes were hot with hurt pride.

'You OK?' asked Chris.

'Sure,' snapped Nicky. 'I nearly tore my ankle off on this damn carpet. Help me up.' Chris lifted his friend from the deck, supporting him under his arm. He started to turn towards their half. 'No,' said Nicky. 'I'm going off. Help me over behind the goal.'

Chris left Nicky to the attentions of the coaches. He noticed that Nicky was up after a minute or so, walking around the touchline with his cousin. Then he lost sight of him.

The last ten minutes passed without any more incidents. The Blues were pressing forward as the ref blew for time, and Chris went over to shake hands with the defenders and wrap a consoling arm round Mac's shoulders.

'Thanks for rubbing it in how short I am,' Mac moaned, but he was obviously pleased with the way he'd played. They walked off together. Chris tried to see where Nicky had limped off to, but he couldn't see him. Perhaps he was getting changed.

Sean Priest walked over towards Chris and beckoned him to step away from the others for a moment.

'Nice game,' he said. 'I expect you found it a bit tougher than the matches you play with the school team?'

'I'll say!'

Priest nodded. 'You don't play with any other team, do you?' Chris shook his head. Priest had a moment's thought about this. 'It might be an idea if you got involved with a local youth team. Some of the coaches here are helping out with a team called Riverside Colts, who train on the college pitches at the university. Would you be interested?'

'Yes! Where – how –?'

'Practice is Wednesdays at six o'clock. If you get picked, matches are Sundays. They play in the Oldcester Youth League, in the First Division. The standard is pretty high –'

'That'll be great!'

'OK. I'll have a word with Iain Walsh next week. He manages the team; he's a good coach too. There's still a few weeks left of the season, so turn up Wednesday week and show him what you can do.'

'Right! I'll be there!'

'Off you go then. I expect I'll see you again.'

Chris ran off to rejoin the others outside the changing rooms on cloud nine. The coaches had some final words for them as a group, but Chris hardly heard any of it. The next thing he knew, they were all running into the changing rooms to hit the showers.

Chris was more weary than he could ever remember. It felt good, though. He knew he'd shown some of his best work that afternoon, and Sean Priest had obviously liked what he'd seen. He couldn't wait to tell Nicky – hopefully his friend would have some good news too.

He didn't find Nicky inside the changing rooms, so once he was dressed he went looking for him outside. The coach who'd looked at his ankle didn't know where he was. Worse, when Chris looked for Paulo's ratty old Chevy, it wasn't where they'd left it.

Could anything else go wrong? he wondered.

'Lost something?' mocked a familiar voice.

Nine

Chris turned, and his heart sank as he came face to face with the loser from Blackmoor advancing towards him across the car park — one face he hadn't wanted to be that close to again.

'Get lost,' he said.

The kid rubbed his hand through a thick mat of blond hair and glared at Chris. Chris was starting to know that look far too well.

'I thought you might be lost, beanpole. Lost or left behind.'

A sick feeling gripped Chris's stomach. 'What do you mean?'

'Your little pal went off in that heap of a car without you. What's the matter, did you and your little boyfriend have a little argument?'

Right then, Chris felt angrier than ever before in his life. Although he didn't want to believe him, he knew that the guy from Blackmoor was telling the truth. Nicky was acting up again. The certainty that this was what was happening flared up inside Chris like a volcano. All at once, he was in the Blackmoor guy's face, remembering how it was this jerk's hand that had ripped the sleeve on his jacket. In that one moment, he forgot how good the day had been, and all the hurt and frustration of the last week or so welled up and boiled over.

'You really are a prat,' he told the guy, and he threw a punch at the side of his head.

Chris had always known he was never going to make it as a boxer, so it came as little surprise when the other lad rocked back from the blow, stunned, but by no means out of it. His hands reached out and gripped Chris's sweatshirt. Though he was probably just a year older, the Blackmoor kid was plenty bigger. Chris felt his trainers lift off the floor.

'I hope you did well in the trial,' the boy snarled into Chris's face. 'It'd be really good to have you turn up every week so that I could do this . . .'

As he finished speaking, he hefted Chris over the bonnet of the nearest car, just missing the wing mirror. Chris landed heavily on the wing, crashing against the thin metal with a thunderous crack. He twisted, and rolled to the ground under the front headlight.

His opponent was already on his way around the wing of the car to continue the dispute, fists clenched. Chris, lying winded on the floor, realised that it would be a long, long run to the cafe in the precinct this time.

'Bennett!' came a loud shout.

Chris looked up. The guy from Blackmoor had fixed his hand in Chris's hair and was in the process of lifting him up for some more aggravation. Chris dangled in his grasp, half-crouching, trying to break free as he was hauled to his feet. To his relief, he realised that Ray Foulds was advancing across the car park towards them.

'What's going on?' the scout demanded.

'This kid just fell over . . . I was helping him up . . .' Bennett lied quickly. It felt funny knowing his name. A pretty ordinary name, too. Chris had always imagined it would be something like Rottweiler. Perhaps that was his first name?

'By his hair?'

Bennett released his grip. 'I didn't want to grab hold of his shirt in case it ripped,' he said, with a cruel grin at Chris.

'Well, I'm sure Mr Stephens is very grateful, aren't you, Chris? Meanwhile, I saw your mother waiting over by the gate, Bennett. Why don't you let her know where you are?'

'Yeah, don't keep mummy waiting,' whispered Chris. He saw Bennett stiffen but there wasn't anything he could do.

'I hope we get the chance to play together again,' the Blackmoor player said, with barely disguised loathing.

'Count on it,' replied Chris.

Bennett left, and Chris stood up, looking around for his bag. It was on the far side of the car. Chris noticed for the first time that it was Foulds' Mondeo. There was a scuff mark on the front wing where Chris had landed.

'Looking for someone, Chris?' asked Foulds.

'Ah, no.'

'Didn't you come with Fiorentini's cousin?'

Chris couldn't believe his bad luck. Foulds had already told him how he thought that Chris and Nicky were a team, two players who worked better together than they did alone. The only two times he had seen them play, they'd ended up arguing over football — assuming that was what this was all about. Chris tried to think of another explanation. No matter how he racked his brains, he could only come up with the one conclusion. Nicky had deliberately left him behind.

'I . . . err . . . think his cousin forgot he was supposed to take me home.'

Foulds gave Chris a look that proved he knew more about what was going on than Chris wanted him to.

'I'll take you back; it's almost on my way. Besides, I want to have a word with you.'

He unlocked the boot for Chris to drop his bag in, then they got into the car. Foulds concentrated on getting out of the crowded car park.

The scout stayed silent until they were the other side of the city centre, moving swiftly along the ring road. Chris stared out of the window at the growing gloom.

'You did well today,' Foulds commented suddenly, almost making Chris jump.

'Did I?'

'Sean Priest is very impressed.'

'He wants me to play with Riverside Colts,' Chris informed him.

'So I hear,' said Foulds, smiling. 'It's an excellent idea.'

They turned off on to the riverside road. The university passed by on the right — Spirebrook was about four miles further on. Chris waited patiently to be told more as the journey continued. Foulds, though, didn't have anything else to say until he was indicating to turn left into Chris's street.

'I told him that you and Nicky always played well together. I think I was proved right today, although Nicky wasn't really himself, was he?'

'I think he's got a bug or something,' Chris replied in a low voice, and he wondered to himself why he was bothering to cover up for Fiorentini's mistakes and moods.

'Ah,' said Foulds, slowing the car to a halt outside Chris's house. Chris waited again. He saw Baynham looking out of the window of the front room. 'You had a good day, though.' Chris thought about that. He knew he'd shown some of his best stuff, but he couldn't forget that it was Nicky's bad luck that had contributed to that fabulous last goal, nor that they had played a blinder together in the second five-a-side. 'When's the county final?' asked Foulds. Chris told him it was Thursday week (the day after he was supposed to turn up at Riverside for the first time!), at 3pm. Mrs Cole was letting them off classes for the afternoon specially. 'I think Sean and I will be coming to watch that. Afterwards, maybe I ought to have a chat with your parents.'

'OK.' Chris could feel his heart beating faster. Funnily enough, though, Foulds didn't look like a man bringing good news.

'Tell me, Chris. Do you want to go up to Manchester?'

Chris hadn't thought about it, not even after his chat with Nicky at school. 'I don't know. Why?'

'Nicky's determined that he wants to go. I've said I'll fix it up. I'd prefer to wait until after the final, but it really depends on what people at Old Trafford say – we may have to go up before. I'll let you know.'

'OK.'

Foulds turned in his seat so that he could look at Chris more directly. He scratched his upper lip. 'You do want to carry on playing with Nicky, don't you? You're still partners, right?'

'I guess so.'

'There aren't any problems?'

'Nothing I know about.' That was nearly true. He could guess what had made Nicky leave him behind at the training ground, but he wanted to hear it from Nicky's mouth before he said anything.

'I'd be sorry if this business split you two up. You overlap really well.' He paused, clearly thinking about that for a moment. 'Yes, it's just like when you get a full back and a winger working together down the touchline. Ordinarily, the full back has a chance against either of them, but put the two together and he's beaten. You and Nicky have such a good understanding, it makes you both better players.'

Chris suddenly thought he saw where this was going. 'Are you saying I'm not good enough to make it on to the youth team on my own?'

Foulds took a long time to answer. 'I'm not saying that. But I think other people might.'

Chris bit his lip. Now it was his turn to think slowly about what he wanted to say. 'Then I'd better come with you and Nicky when you go up to Old Trafford, hadn't I?'

'Are you sure that's what you want?'

Chris looked down at his sweatshirt. It was an Oldcester shirt, in the club colours and with the club badge on the breast. During the trial, he'd been wearing the club's colours, just like most of the other boys (Nicky had chosen a plain blue shirt, probably part of his campaign not to appear too interested). Oldcester was the only team Chris had ever supported; the only one he'd ever dreamed of playing for.

'I'm sure,' he said.

⚽

Chris's father seemed OK with the news that he wanted to go up to Manchester with Nicky. He wasn't as excited about the way things were turning out as Chris might have expected, but Chris put it down to his father being disappointed that he'd had to work on the day of the trial.

Later, when Foulds went round to confirm that he'd fixed things for Chris and Nicky to visit Old Trafford before the county final, Chris listened as his father checked all the arrangements. His voice sounded quite flat.

Pete Baynham was round at Griff's house, so they had the place to themselves. Chris finished his homework and went down to find his father watching some old film about the Roman Empire on the TV.

'What's all this about?' asked Chris. He didn't recognise any of the actors, although some of them were supposed to be quite famous.

'Alec Guinness is the Roman Emperor. He's dying, and he has to choose who will take over. That guy is his adopted

60

son; his real son is a nasty bit of work. He chooses the adopted son.'

'Oh.' Chris sat and watched a bit of the film. He was a bit confused because he'd always thought Romans wore togas or armour and red cloaks. These guys were wearing heavy, brown cloaks. There were a couple of good fights, but otherwise he couldn't really get interested.

'So, who wins in the end?'

'The good guy, of course. The real son gets killed.'

Chris uttered a small laugh. 'Are you trying to tell me something?'

His dad turned to look at him, his face adopting the confused expression it usually wore when Chris made one of his jokes.

'What?'

'Are you going to adopt Pete and give him my season ticket?'

His dad laughed, then picked up the remote and killed the TV. 'Would you mind?'

'Of course!'

'Oh. Only I wasn't sure if you still supported Oldcester any more.'

Now it was Chris's turn to be confused. 'What?'

'Well, there's this business with Manchester United, and you going up there at the weekend. What's brought that on?'

Chris shrugged. He still wasn't sure why he was going himself. He certainly couldn't explain it.

His father turned round in his seat a little more so that he could look Chris squarely in the eyes. Chris uttered a small groan inside; this was usually a sign that his father wanted to have a serious chat about something. Last time it had been about his jacket.

'Chris, you know I'm happy with the idea of you becoming a footballer. I might not have chosen it myself, but you've always been good enough, in my opinion, and I know you enjoy playing. I've always said that so long as you work hard at school and pass your exams I'd be as pleased as punch if you made the grade.' He took a moment to collect his thoughts. 'Truth is, I'm more proud of you than I've let on. It's quite a buzz for me, watching you get better each year. You've always seemed to know exactly where you were going. So I suppose I'm just a bit surprised that you're not more interested in trying to get into the set-up at Oldcester. From what you said about the trial, and now this business with Riverside, they like you. I just don't see where Manchester fits into the picture. I don't see how it can work.'

'I'm only going for a look,' replied Chris. 'It doesn't mean anything. And besides, it's not like we're just going to up sticks and move to Manchester, is it?'

His father searched his face, clearly looking for some clue that Chris really meant what he said. In the end, he just smiled, and reached for the remote again. 'You're too good for Man U anyway . . .' he said.

Chris laughed and settled back to see just what did happen to the Emperor's son.

Ten

⚽

Chris and Nicky had really been...

Foulds picked Chris up early the following Saturday, then they drove off to get Nicky. There was some delay while Foulds argued with Uncle Fabian about something on the doorstep while the boys waited in the car.

'I told Uncle Fabian I didn't want him to come,' chuckled Nicky.

'Why not?' asked Chris.

'It's just a look around, nothing else. If Uncle Fabian comes along, he'll try to get me into the first team for the match.'

Chris laughed. Nicky was in a really good mood. He showed Chris a bag of supplies his mother had packed. Somehow, the subject of Nicky's disappearance after the trial just didn't come up — just the way it had been avoided all week at school.

Chris had nearly said something during practice on Tuesday, but he didn't want to spoil what turned out to be a cracking session. On Thursday, they had played a Schools League game against South Weston, and won 6–0. Again, Nicky had been in top form, and had supplied Chris with enough chances to score a dozen goals.

It was as if the trial had never happened, and Chris couldn't see any point in nagging Nicky about leaving him behind. The last thing he wanted was to set Nicky off again.

On the motorway, Foulds played a CD of some dreadful eighties rock band, which made Chris and Nicky squirm in agony. Nicky had his CD Walkman, and insisted they needed to listen to Blur or Pulp to get over the nausea caused by Talking Feet (or whatever they were called).

The journey flew by and they reached Manchester in plenty of time. As they drove towards Old Trafford, the boys gasped at the sheer number of people heading the same way, all kitted out in red and white.

'What are this lot doing here? United don't have a home game this afternoon. They go to Chelsea tomorrow.'

'It's not the first team. The reserves are playing.'

'The reserves?!' the boys cried in unison.

'Giggs is playing this afternoon, now that he's over his injury, and there's been a rumour that some of the young lads who have been playing in the first team will be given a run too. They're expecting twenty thousand this afternoon.'

'Twenty thousand?!'

'Could be.'

'Looks more like a hundred and twenty thousand to me,' Nicky observed, twisting in every direction to see the crowds. 'How can this lot all fit in?'

'Old Trafford's a big place, Nicky. You'll see.'

Chris and Nicky had rarely been to a game in front of such a large crowd, and certainly not for a reserve game! Star Park only had a capacity of 24,000, and there weren't many games that attracted more than 18,000. Chris had been up to Elland Road and there had been 27,000 there, but this was something else!

It took ages to get to the ground and ages to park. Everything seemed huge, and they felt quite lost in the sheer size and scale of everything. Even the queues at the hamburger stand were bigger than anything they'd ever known!

Foulds showed a pass at the gate and they stepped inside. He led them towards a door at the base of one of the huge stands. A uniformed steward checked his pass again.

They were met by one of the youth team coaches, a smartly dressed young man who shook them by the hands and whisked them into a smart lounge for a drink and a chat.

'Ray's told me quite a lot about you. We're very proud of our youth team policy here at Old Trafford, and we're always looking for the best young players. We get quite a few lads like you coming up and having a look around. Over the summer, we'll have a few of you in to show us what they can do. Then, if you make the grade, we'd talk to you about signing youth forms – but I expect Ray's already told you all about the legal side of things, right?' They nodded. 'You're both Oldcester United fans, I hear?' They nodded again. Chris couldn't help looking out of the window. They were looking out over the city. It seemed vast compared to Oldcester. 'Think you'll avoid the drop?'

'No problem,' said Chris, confidently. Nicky said nothing.

'You've got some big games coming up. We come down to you on Wednesday. Will you be there? It'll be a bad one for you to lose.'

Chris shrugged. 'We'll make it,' he said.

They talked a bit more about football, and school and family and other things. The guy talked to them about how they worked things at Old Trafford, but Chris had trouble taking it all in.

'Of course, if you did sign for us, you'd be a long way from home.'

'I'm not bothered,' said Nicky, grinning. 'Our house is too full anyway. And my auntie lives just outside Bolton. I could stay with her.'

'That's you sorted, then!' The young man laughed. 'What about you, Chris?'

'I dunno,' Chris admitted. And he realised then that he felt completely lost in this place, far from home.

'Well, that's not a problem. That's why you're here, after all, so we can meet up, have a chat, and see if there are things that need sorting out.'

That pretty well completed the business of their trip. The young man stood up, straightened his suit and checked his watch. 'I'll have to leave you now,' he said. 'I have a coaching clinic for the Under-18s in twenty minutes, and I need to get changed. But Ray's an old friend here; he'll show you round. Stay for the game if you like. And I'll be in touch about you coming to see us again during the summer, OK?'

They shook hands again and then he was gone. Foulds looked at them both. Nicky was beaming widely. Chris still felt a bit strange.

'Come on,' said Foulds. 'Let's have a sneak around.'

The stands were full of restaurants and conference rooms and executive suites. There were as many flights of stairs as in a skyscraper. Foulds led them down into the depths.

'Follow me,' said Foulds, stepping through the doors at the

far end of a long, brightly lit passage. Chris and Nicky followed him through, and then stopped in the doorway as if they'd been freeze-framed. Neither of them dared set foot in the space beyond.

The room was bright, and much larger than they could have imagined. On one side there was a huge bath. Along another wall there were lockers – not battered old cabinets with rusty doors like the boys were used to, but smart, brightly painted lockers – with locks.

Spaced around the walls, above a wide wooden bench, the boys saw ten bright red shirts hanging from pegs, each with its number facing into the room. Above each peg, a small card bore the name of the man who would wear the shirt in just another few hours. Butt, Scholes, Neville – it was like looking at a team sheet in a programme or a page in a football sticker album. And this was a reserve team!

Right at the end, the No. 11 shirt had a card above it with the word 'Giggs' in smart black lettering.

'Awesome,' said Nicky.

After letting them gawk for a few minutes, Foulds passed into the passage beyond the doors and the boys reluctantly left the dressing room. At once, they realised where they were now; daylight was streaming down from one end of the passage and they could see bright plastic seats and smell clean, new-mown grass.

Foulds led the way up the tunnel and they emerged into the sun. 'I don't believe this . . .' Chris whispered.

Lush green grass stretched away in front of them, while all around the stands rose like vast walls, filled with row after row of red seats. Thousand upon thousand. Even though the stadium was vast, each seat seemed close enough to touch, and Chris could hear the swelling roar of the fans in his mind. What would it be like to step out on to Old Trafford's turf with 40,000 fans cheering your arrival?

Nicky was still walking ahead of him, his attention fixed on the goal to his left. A large, blond-haired giant was patrolling between the posts, taking gentle strikes into his arms and sliding the ball back out to the black-haired outfield player who stood on the penalty spot. Flicking the ball up, he volleyed the ball back to his green-shirted companion. The

66

drill was so quick, the ball was almost a blur passing back and forth between them.

'It's –' began Nicky, but he couldn't actually say their names. Foulds laughed. 'Come and say hello,' he said.

They crossed the park, and it felt like their feet weren't even disturbing the grass. From the edge of the box, Foulds called to the two players. 'Ryan, Peter . . . do you have a minute?'

The dark-haired player ended the drill by firing the ball into the net. The keeper frowned briefly, but then they both stepped forward, wearing wide smiles. Foulds made the introductions, gesturing quickly. 'Chris Stephens, Nicky Fiorentini, meet Ryan Giggs and Peter Schmeichel.'

Nicky clearly wasn't able to say anything, but Chris managed to choke out, 'Hi!' The two stars shook his hand.

'Where are you two from?' asked Ryan.

'Oldcester,' croaked Chris.

'Is that right? I'm hoping Alex will let me play you lot on Wednesday. Maybe I'll see you down there.'

'You both play for the same school?' Schmeichel said, spinning the ball in his hands. Chris nodded. 'You any good?' Chris nodded again. Schmeichel laughed. 'They're lucky to have you both at the same time.'

The boys managed to laugh back feebly. Chris tried to get his brain and his mouth working at the same time, but he couldn't manage to find anything to say.

'They're just getting the tour,' Foulds explained to the two players. 'How's the ankle, Ryan?'

'Good. Alex wants me to try it out; see if I'm ready to come back into the first team on Wednesday.'

'They've missed you,' said Foulds. Giggs smiled. 'Nicky's a winger,' Foulds continued, pointing him out. 'He's almost as fast as you. If we can just get him to work a bit harder than you do he might make a half-decent player.'

The two players laughed, Schmeichel in particular. 'Don't you ever give up?' asked Ryan.

Foulds shrugged and bent to whisper into Nicky's ear. 'He's inclined to slack off when I'm not here to keep an eye on him.'

The big goalkeeper was looking restless. 'You want to knock a few balls around?' he asked. Chris nodded.

'We don't have any kit . . .' muttered Nicky.

'They don't want you to play this afternoon, Nicky,' said Foulds, grinning. 'It's just a little work-out . . .'

Chris bent down and tightened the laces on his trainers. There was no way he was going to miss out on an opportunity like this. He stepped forward quickly.

'I'm game,' he said.

Schmeichel retreated back towards the goal-line. 'Take a few shots from the edge of the box,' he instructed Chris, setting himself up. Foulds picked up a bag of balls and stood over to one side, spreading the balls in a row at his feet. Chris stepped to the edge of the box.

Foulds knocked the balls across the box, one by one. Chris almost died when he spooned the first one high and wide, but then he balanced himself more solidly on the next one and put it high to Schmeichel's left. For a moment, he thought it was goal bound, but the keeper took off from his left foot and parried the ball with his hands.

'Don't stop . . . keep them coming . . .' the keeper instructed, springing up as soon as he landed. Foulds ferried the balls in faster and Chris unleashed a barrage of twelve shots. Ten were on target; Schmeichel got to them all.

'Not bad,' said the big keeper, grinning, as he knocked the last ball back to Chris's feet. Chris was amazed. Two or three of those shots would have beaten anyone he had ever faced, but the United keeper had made them all look easy.

Foulds rolled a ball back three or four yards outside the box. 'Hit a free kick from there, Chris,' he said.

Chris took six or seven paces back, then ran in fast. He struck the ball with the outside of his right boot and it bent away as Schmeichel took off to his left. The big keeper was left grasping for air as the ball kissed the inside of the post and went in.

'Nice!' Ryan called admiringly from the side.

Schmeichel looked up from the ground. 'That's easy for him to say . . .' he muttered.

Ryan and Nicky had wandered off to one side, and they took it in turn to try and take the ball past the other at speed. Nicky was left floundering; Giggs did him every time. Once or twice, Nicky had the United winger in return. A few spectators on that side cheered.

68

'Good!' Ryan called after him the second time. 'Don't make your first move too obvious . . . keep the defender guessing. As soon as he shifts one way, that's when you need to change pace. Try again.'

Meanwhile, Foulds threw a few balls in for Chris to meet in the air. He managed to beat Schmeichel twice, directing the ball down sharply from just outside the six-yard box. 'You're good in the air,' muttered the keeper, picking the second one from the net.

After twenty minutes or so, they stopped. 'I have to go,' said Giggs. 'Kick-off's in just over an hour.'

Peter punched Chris on the shoulder. 'Pretty good, kid!' he said, grinning. Chris grinned back.

Out on the touchline, Nicky looked up, and instantly struck the ball towards the open goal. Blindingly quickly, Schmeichel dropped the ball he was holding, ran back three steps, and tipped the shot over the bar.

'Wingers, eh?' the Dane called loudly, gesturing to Nicky with his thumb down. 'Ever since Nayim did Seaman like that, they all think they can beat you from fifty yards.'

After a few moments, clearly wondering how on earth the ball hadn't ended up in the back of the net, Nicky jogged over. The boys thanked the two United players. Chris asked for their autographs, then realised he didn't have so much as a bus ticket for them to write on. Giggs signed Chris's trainers with a marker Foulds had in his pocket. Someone threw Schmeichel a programme, and he signed that.

'Bring that with you on Wednesday, and come and say hello. I'll tell someone in the office to let you in, provided you don't tell people you beat me twice in the air.'

Giggs jogged off, waving to the people who were already in the ground. Their cheers echoed in the vast stands.

Foulds turned to Nicky. 'Didn't you want their autographs as well?'

Nicky shook his head. 'When you're a United player, you don't go asking all the other United players for autographs.' Nicky turned a hand-spring on the grass. 'This is fantastic!' he yelled, and the shout echoed around Old Trafford. The early arrivals cheered back.

Eleven

The next week was all about getting ready for the county final. Chris tried to concentrate in class but it was a struggle. By Monday lunchtime, he'd almost forgotten about the visit to Manchester.

Nicky, though, was always there to remind him. He sat at the centre of an excited group of kids at break, telling them about the visit. Even Fuller was listening without interruption.

'Schmeichel came and sat with us during the game. He says he likes to see how the reserves are playing because so many of them find their way into the first team. They took Southampton to the cleaners. It was embarrassing to watch.'

'It was only two-nil,' argued Chris.

'Oh, right, like that third goal should have been disallowed. Giggs was never offside.'

Chris decided he might as well stay quiet. This was Nicky's story, and he didn't have to play a large part in it, along with the rest of the real world.

'Giggs hit this one shot from forty yards . . . it was just wide. Then Butt banged a header in from the edge of the box, and Paul Scholes got the second. I thought he'd mucked it up because he tried to dummy the goalkeeper too early, but it went in off his body.'

Chris knew that Nicky was already scoring goals for Manchester United in his head that would put Scholes' effort to shame. He'd talked about that kick-about session as if it was part of the game. 'Giggs thought I was going left, but I stepped over the ball and pulled it across him just as he was stretching to make the tackle . . .'

'So, do they want you to go up there?' asked Griff, much more interested in the realities of everyday life. He was still asking when Nicky was getting his £10,000.

'We have to go up to a training camp thing in August, but I reckon it's a foregone conclusion. We were the best players at the trial at Oldcester. I reckon Foulds will have told them they've got to take us.'

Chris was starting to find Nicky's swelled head irritating. Not wanting to say anything he might regret, he walked off to get a drink.

Pete Baynham followed him over. 'Was it as good as Nicky says?'

Chris tried to think carefully about his answer. He'd had a brilliant day, but there was a big difference in the way he remembered it. Nicky wanted to play in that vast arena every week. Inside Chris, there was just this gnawing desire to play there in a blue and red shirt; to lead Oldcester on to the pitch with that huge crowd roaring, and then to score the winning goal as —

'You wouldn't be in red and blue. You'd be away. Manchester wear red at home, so you'd have to be in blue and white.'

Chris started. Had he really said all that out loud? Pete was looking at him as if he was cracking up.

'Nicky says we ought to practise tonight, as well as Tuesday.'

'Fine.'

'Wednesday too, he says.'

'We can't Wednesday.'

'Oh, why not?'

'We have to be somewhere,' said Chris. He wasn't sure why he was being so vague, but a strange sense of unease was crawling over him. He didn't believe for a moment that Nicky would forget something like an invitation to play with Riverside Colts. Which meant . . .

Baynham didn't ask for any more details, so Chris was content to let the matter drop. After school, he and Nicky borrowed the key to the equipment locker from Flea, dragging out the practice balls, the five-a-side goals and the cones. They set them up in the playground.

'Closer together, remember,' Nicky told Chris.

Chris was on the point of telling Nicky that he doubted that some of their team could run between cones that closely

71

grouped without tripping over, never mind dribbling a ball, but he saw how determined Nicky was to bring all their recent experiences back to the rest of the guys.

The others assembled slowly — Baynham, Mac, Griff, Fuller, Doughnut, Packham. Not quite such magical names as those they had seen at Old Trafford, but the best that Spirebrook could offer. The others watched as Chris and Nicky started a drill, each running up one side of the line of cones, hitting first-time passes through the spaces.

Every pass was pin-point accurate. Griff and Fuller tried to copy them, but the first pass cannoned off one of the cones, and Fuller was sent chasing after it.

'Concentrate!' called Nicky from the far end. 'Keep your passes accurate.'

They set up one of the five-a-side goals at one end of the line so that at the end of the drill one of each pair could take a shot on goal. Nicky fed Chris perfectly every time, but Baynham was barely troubled by the rest of the team.

'They're not concentrating!' moaned Nicky. Chris wondered how often he was going to use that word tonight before somebody clouted him.

'You and me should split up,' said Chris.

They gave that a go. Chris buddied up with Javinder Ray, a recent arrival at Spirebrook, who was on the verge of making it into the team once one of the older boys moved up. Javinder was light on his feet, and very quick. He and Chris moved quickly down the line, and it was only the last pass that went off target.

Nicky picked Fuller, which proved to be a big mistake. Fuller wasn't a natural passer of the ball; he saw his job as making tackles in midfield and leaving it to the 'pretty' players to do something with the possession he won.

After two or three fluffed runs, Fuller showed what he was best at by kicking one of the cones twenty yards up the pitch.

Nicky next tried to organise a couple of laps of the pitch, but no-one was buying any real exercise on a cool, damp spring evening, and they certainly weren't ready to take orders from Nicky.

'One lap, then!' he said, getting under everyone's skin.

'Who put you in charge?' complained Griff, who was, after

all, team captain, and a year older than Nicky.

'This is the kind of stuff they do at real football clubs.'

'So what?'

'So we should do it better. We've got to be a lot fitter, a lot more –'

Griff took a long, fast stride towards Nicky and stood in front of him. He was a lot taller than Nicky and almost had to bend down to look him in the eye. Nicky looked up hesitantly, perhaps realising that he'd gone too far.

'Listen, Nicky – we've all just about had it with you and your trial and your day out at Manchester United. We've always practised the same way, and we made it through to the county final just fine. So lighten up, OK?'

Nicky opened his mouth, but clearly thought better of trying to convince Griff. He smiled up at the team captain as he replied.

'OK, fine. We'll beat East Sheils anyway. We're getting together tomorrow as normal, right?'

'That's right,' said Griff, nodding.

'What about Wednesday?' asked Nicky.

'I thought Wednesday was off,' said Baynham, standing off to the side with a puzzled look on his face.

Chris felt a cold hand clutch his heart. He knew at once what was about to happen, but it was like seeing a few pebbles fall and knowing that he was under the path of an avalanche. He couldn't stop it; he couldn't get away from it. He just had to get buried.

'Why's that?' asked Nicky.

'Chris can't make it, for one,' said Baynham.

'Nor me,' came a voice from the back, which sounded like Mac's. Chris didn't turn to find out. Nicky was peering out from under the shadow of Griff's bulk.

'Where are you going Wednesday?'

Chris tried to think quickly, but his brain was sluggish. 'Star Park . . . you know, the Manchester game.'

'Duh!' mocked Nicky. 'I know! But it's an eight o'clock kick-off. We can easy get in two hours before.'

'I can't,' came Mac's voice (it was definitely him).

'Yeah, but I have to go and see someone as well.'

Nicky emerged from under Griff's arm and faced Chris.

'Who?'

'I'm going to see the bloke in charge of Riverside Colts,' Mac's voice piped from the rear. Chris looked over his shoulder this time. Mac was explaining their plans to Fuller. It was Nicky, though, who was all ears. 'That Ray Foulds guy fixed it up, didn't he, Chris?' Mac continued. 'Said it would help if we played for more than one team, against some different opposition. I'm going to see if I can play outfield for a change.'

Nicky's eyes took on the quality of dark glass. The wind tugged at his tousled black hair, whipping it across his forehead.

'Riverside? They're a youth club or something, aren't they?'

'That's right!' Mac said cheerfully, happy to see that Nicky was curious even if Fuller wasn't. 'Only they've got this football team as well that plays over on the university pitches. Foulds has fixed it up for Chris and me to go along on Wednesday and see if we can get in.' Mac's voice trailed to a close, clearly aware just how chilled the air had become over the last ten seconds. 'Some of the Oldcester coaches run it . . .' he finished lamely, before joining the silence centred around where Nicky was facing Chris.

'I thought you knew,' said Chris at last. 'I just assumed they'd asked you to play as well . . .'

Nicky didn't answer. His face was almost bright red, as if he was going to explode. Chris could feel that something that had once been very strong was about to be destroyed for ever.

Before he could say another word, Nicky stormed off. It was so fast, no-one even managed to blink an eyelid between Nicky just being there, his face clouding over, and then him being ten metres away, disappearing fast.

'Nicky!' called Chris. The gap increased. He called again, but Nicky broke into a run. Chris circled off to the side, grabbed both their bags, and set off in pursuit. Mac and Fuller stepped aside as he rushed past. Mac tried to say something but Chris didn't pause even for a second.

'What – are we supposed to put all this stuff away then?' cried Griff.

Twelve

In the movies, when the bad guy whacks Steven Seagal or Arnie or Sly over the head, he's left unconscious for an hour, then he comes round, rubs a small graze a couple of times (wincing slightly), and two seconds later he's ready to save the world once more.

It was Chris's painful pleasure to discover that when his wits started to recover, his skull was throbbing like it had been smacked hard with an iron bar. Which was more or less what had happened, except that he'd hit the metal, not the other way around.

He was lying on the cold stone of the jetty, barely a foot from the edge. There was a loud ringing noise in the back of his head. Behind his shoulders, he could feel something very solid. He turned his head — which caused the splitting pain to sharpen for a second — and saw that he had ended up against one of the bollards. That was what had dented his head.

He remembered dreaming vividly about the events of the last few weeks, but the pictures were fading now. Strangely, except for the sparks that were flashing in front of his eyes, Chris found he could actually see through the gloom a little better than he could before. Turning away from the river, he saw Nicky standing against the wall of the bridge, his fists clenched, his teeth grinding together and his whole body rigid with fury. There was a small recess in the wall. Nicky must have been hiding in it when Chris ran past.

'Nicky . . .' croaked Chris. It was hard to concentrate.

'Why are you following me?' yelled Nicky, his voice echoing. Chris tried to sit up but he still felt a little woozy. 'Come to gloat? Come to have a good laugh?' Chris wanted to tell Nicky that the last thing he wanted to do right now was laugh, but the words wouldn't come. 'I can't believe you did this to me!' Nicky yelled, his voice becoming even louder and more shrill.

'I did to you?' gasped Chris.

'Don't pretend! I knew right off that you were going to this thing on Wednesday. You didn't have to say a thing. I just knew!' Nicky had started pacing back and forth, a short route that kept him in the bridge's dark shadow. Chris found following him with his eyes really painful, so he stopped turning his head and kept still. 'I thought we were mates! But I can see now you had this planned all along. As soon as Foulds came along, you started doing everything you could to make yourself look good, even if it made me look bad. You stole that goal in the semi-final, sucked up to the coaches in the trial . . . and now it's paid off, has it? Foulds wants you to play for his pet team?'

'Wait a minute . . . that's not what happened!'

'What about Man United, eh?' Nicky cried, drowning Chris's objections. 'I fixed it up for you to come with me!' Chris was starting to shake off the worst effects of the hit now, and sat up, resting his back against the iron bollard. He felt quite sick. 'See the difference?' Nicky ranted. 'I have something good happen to me; I share it with you. You get something good happen – oh, look! You keep it to yourself!'

'But I thought –'

'I can't believe I trusted you,' Nicky said, and he bent suddenly to pick up his bag from where it had fallen. 'I won't make that mistake again.' Nicky's face became very sharp and hard. When he spoke, the words tumbled out like gunfire. 'Uncle Fabian has spoken to Old Trafford again. I'm going to go up there in the summer, stay with my aunt, and get myself into their youth team. I don't need you, Chris. I never did.'

And with that he ran off, briefly lit by the daylight as he moved out from under the bridge, but then he clambered up the embankment and disappeared. Chris heard his footsteps for a few minutes longer, and then there was nothing.

It took him a long time to pull his thoughts together.

Nicky was so far off the mark that Chris couldn't think where to start explaining it to himself, let alone how to try and make Nicky see sense. Nicky had been the one desperate to impress Foulds; he'd been the one who had gone off on his own with the Manchester thing. Chris had just been caught up in his wake, even when it didn't make sense to follow Nicky's lead. This whole, stupid mess was all Nicky's fault!

So why was he the bad guy?

After a while, Chris found that he could stand, and he pulled himself from the jetty and staggered away from the edge. The last haunting echoes of his dreams of the past dropped away. Then he remembered his bag. He turned to look round but it wasn't there. The memory of a dull splash came back into his mind.

'Oh no!'

He could see the marks he'd made in the dirt as he skidded over the ground. That was when it struck him. If he hadn't hit the bollard, nothing would have stopped him following his bag into the river.

Realising what might have happened hurt Chris even more than when Nicky had smashed into him, or when his head had hit the bollard. The truth was he could have been killed.

Thirteen

There wasn't anything good to say about the next few days. Chris's father had whisked him straight to hospital. Possible concussion, they said, suggesting a week of rest.

'But the trial with the Colts; the match with United; the final!'

Chris's protests were swept aside. The Colts could wait a week; missing one home game wouldn't kill him; they'd see how he felt on Thursday before they decided about the final.

Only when he knew Chris was going to suffer nothing worse than a bump the size of an egg and a roaring headache did his father ask what had happened. Chris told a version of the truth; he'd had an argument with Nicky and he'd fallen and hit his head. He didn't mention the fact that they had finished the argument on the old chemical works' site – his father would have had kittens.

It sounded lame even as he said it, but his father hadn't challenged the story at all.

That had been bad enough, but it got worse. Pete Baynham arrived home in floods of tears on Tuesday. Nicky had persuaded Flea that they had to play Mac in goal for the final. Having spent all this time away from his mum, Pete was going to spend the game on the bench. Chris knew the decision made sense, but it seemed a desperately hard thing to do to Pete.

And worse. A teacher had seen Chris going over the fence and reported it to the head teacher. Mrs Cole wanted to see him as soon as he was fit enough to go back to school. The rumour was that Chris was going to be carpeted in a big way.

And worse. Nicky was leaving the school; going to live with

his aunt near Bolton. After this last game, the old partnership was going to split up.

'That must have been some argument,' Chris's father commented.

Thursday morning dawned, bright and clear. Chris woke, feeling better than at any time over the last few days. He threw back the covers on his bed, jumped to the floor and pulled open the curtains. He blinked as the bright light struck his face, and slowly opened his eyes. To his relief, the dull ache in his head had gone.

He dressed, searched through his room for a few items he thought he might need (placing them in a ratty old bag he'd abandoned at Christmas), then made his way downstairs. Baynham was already munching his way through his customary third slice of toast (boiled egg and cereal having preceded it), while Chris's father read the paper and tried to ignore the loud jingles of *The Big Breakfast* rattling the speaker of the portable TV.

'Look what's crept out of the pit,' said Baynham.

Chris's dad peered over the top of the *Daily Express*. His brows lowered in a slight frown: Chris was in his school uniform and he had dumped his kit bag by the kitchen door. The frown lifted with nothing said, and his father disappeared back behind the paper. Chris breathed a sigh of relief. His father sometimes used silence like a weapon; today it meant that he didn't object to the idea of Chris going back to school.

Chris looked at the paper and saw the back page headline which read 'RYAN'S SLAUGHTER'. He'd listened to the game on the radio. Manchester United had run rampant over Oldcester, with Giggs scoring a hat-trick. Schmeichel had saved a penalty, the closest Oldcester had come all night.

'Just as well we didn't go,' Chris commented.

His dad folded the paper back and tossed the paper over for him to read the inside report. 'Five-nil,' he sighed, 'and apparently it wasn't that close.' He poured some tea, putting a steaming mug in front of Chris and then topping up his own. Baynham looked up hopefully, his mug extended.

'Everton won, so they're safe. It looks like us, Southampton or Chelsea to go down with City,' said Chris's father, now crossing the room to the fridge. He pulled out a bottle of silver top, shook it, then placed the bottle, a bowl and a box of cornflakes in front of Chris. 'Not a good night for poor old United,' he added. 'So, I'd better let you win this cup this afternoon or we'll all be suicidal.'

He glanced at Baynham, who was still holding out his mug. He tutted but poured their house guest some more tea anyway.

Far from being suicidal, Baynham was in a very excitable mood now that he'd become used to the idea of not playing. 'Are you letting Chris play, Mr Stephens?'

'Do I have a choice?'

'All right!' laughed Baynham, and he banged his hand on the table so hard that the cutlery jumped. 'Tough break, East Sheils!'

Chris started to eat. His father was looking through his pockets for something. Then he pointed to a carrier bag over on the counter.

'Martin Kemble brought that round for you last night,' he said. Martin was a friend of the family, who was also a steward at Star Park. 'There's a note,' he added.

Chris found the note folded in two and attached to the bag with adhesive tape. On the outside, in block capitals, it just said 'CHRIS'.

He pulled it off, puzzled by the unfamiliar writing. He unfolded it, scanned the note quickly, then read it again:

'I hear you were sick and couldn't make the game. Just as well – you'd have felt really ill if you saw what we did to you! Maybe you can come and see us again – next time you're in the Premiership. Meanwhile, these are for you and your mate. You should be able to work out which is which.'

It took a moment for him to decipher the signature, until he realised it was two names. 'Peter and Ryan.'

He upended the bag. He knew what was in it instantly. Two bright red shirts tumbled on to the breakfast counter. Chris saw some black marks on the surface and realised that each had been signed by the whole Manchester United first team. And he did work out which was which – one was a No. 11

shirt with the word 'GIGGS' printed on the back across the shoulders. The other had no printed name, but in the same black marker with which the shirt had been signed, the word 'SCHMEICHEL' had been written where the name would be. It had probably been another number eleven, but one of the '1's had been removed. To complete the joke, the keeper had written a message above his autograph. 'I didn't think you'd wear a goalie's jersey.'

There was also a PS. It read: '5–0. Ho ho.'

'Brilliant,' said Chris, and he laughed out loud. He showed the note to his father and Baynham. Pete thought the shirt had been ruined and it took a while for Chris to explain what the messages meant. Even then Pete didn't really get it.

'The other one's for Nicky, then?' his father asked.

'Uh-huh,' replied Chris, quietly. 'It's OK,' he added.

He packed the shirts in with his kit, then finished his breakfast. Baynham went off to find his kit.

'Take it easy today,' Chris's father said, recovering the newspaper.

'I will.'

'Don't even think of heading the ball.'

Chris laughed. 'Sure. Are you going to be able to come?'

'I've missed every other game this season and you've won them all. Are you sure my being there won't bring you bad luck?'

'I'll risk it.'

'Good. I'll sneak off work at three.'

Baynham returned and they got ready to leave. 'You know the head wants to see you,' he reminded Chris.

'I know.'

'Still, it's not like she's going to stop you playing tonight, is it? The whole school wants to see us win.'

'We'd better not let them down, then,' said Chris, hoisting his bag over his shoulder.

❂

'You've let everyone down,' said the head.

Chris remained perfectly still, and waited for the verdict. The head had been talking now for about five minutes. Chris was starting to feel that this wasn't going to be as comfortable as he'd hoped.

'You understand the gravity of the situation, don't you, Chris?' she said. As always, Mrs Cole looked very smart and deadly serious. Chris had never known her to make a joke or crack a smile. She had her elbows on her desk and her hands clasped in front of her like a politician or a preacher on the TV. Her face was a mask of seriousness, while her eyes peered at him through her smart, gold-rimmed spectacles. 'That old plant used to process all sorts of chemicals. Many of them were probably highly toxic. Just because all the machinery has been dismantled and the place was cleaned up before the school was built, it doesn't mean it isn't still dangerous in there. They keep finding all kinds of problems – that's why the supermarket still hasn't been built.'

'I didn't know that,' said Chris, and then he added quickly, 'about the supermarket, I mean.'

'Yes, well,' said Mrs Cole, in that way that teachers use when you've scored a real own goal. She was looking down at his school record. At least, thought Chris, there couldn't be any complaint there. 'Ms Robinson says there's been some problem over homework,' Mrs Cole observed.

'I lost some work,' Chris replied. 'I've caught up now.'

'Yes, well . . .' Two-nil! Chris suspected that if he had a hat-trick against him, that would be his lot. 'Then there are books that were "lost" in the river,' Mrs Cole continued. 'They'll have to be replaced.'

'I'm going to get a job over the Easter holidays to earn some money,' Chris informed her.

That merited nothing worse than a 'I see'.

Mrs Cole looked up. 'I'm not a complete convert to the importance of competitive team games,' she said, 'but the National Curriculum places an obligation on teachers to encourage students to take part in sports. The LEA is very keen on inter-school competitions. However, I don't allow that to interfere with the rest of school life. Specifically, I don't allow students to play for the school when they break the rules, or when they allow it to affect their work. I have to tell you, Chris, that I have very seriously considered barring you from playing this afternoon.' Chris felt a lurch in his stomach.

Surely, she didn't mean — 'But I am advised by Mr Lea that this would involve punishing ten other boys for your mistake. I don't believe that's fair.'

'No, Mrs Cole.'

She closed the file and leaned forward over the desk.

'So, instead, I'm going to tell Mr Lea that you are not to be selected again for any school team after today. That will apply for the rest of this term and all the summer term. We'll review the situation after the summer vacation. Is that clear?'

'Yes, Mrs Cole.'

'Any more problems like this, Chris, and I'll suspend you from school. There will be no more warnings.'

'Yes, Mrs Cole.'

Chris remained still for a moment longer to make sure she was finished, then he got up and went to the door.

'Chris . . .' He turned to face the head teacher once more. 'Good luck this afternoon,' she said, smiling ever so slightly.

Chris thanked her and made his escape through the door before she could think of anything else. Outside, he leaned against the wall and breathed a sigh of relief. That might have been a lot worse. Maybe things were going to turn out OK after all.

Fourteen

Of course, compared to dealing with Spirebrook's 'Dragon Lady', facing Nicky wasn't going to be anything like so much fun.

They sat apart during the morning classes, and Nicky disappeared as soon as the lunch bell rang. Although Chris felt that he and Nicky really needed to talk about what had happened, he didn't want to have to face it yet, and it was clear that Nicky was going to avoid a confrontation too. Still, something was gnawing at him like toothache.

He considered trying to track Nicky down but he was intercepted in the playground by other members of the team. Griff, Fuller, Packham and Steve Marsh were circling the playground slowly, talking listlessly together, when they saw Chris and called him over.

'You're back then,' said Griff.

Chris made a point of reading the name tag attached to the inside pocket of his jacket. 'Yes, it's me all right.'

Griff made a face back at him. 'How did it go with "Andy" Cole?' asked Fuller, who liked a bit of drama, particularly if it meant someone else was in trouble.

'OK,' replied Chris. 'She banned me for the rest of the season.' Four jaws dropped open. 'After today,' added Chris, realising what he'd said. Fuller heaved a sigh of relief.

'Well, we weren't going to win the League anyway,' re-marked Griff. 'So long as you're fit to play today.'

'I'm OK.'

The others all nodded. They looked quite relieved. Fuller, though, with his unerring instinct for disaster, knew that there was still more to come.

'So, what's the score with Nicky, then?'

Chris felt his spirits sink. In wondering how today might go, he'd thought about actually facing Nicky, about dealing with Mrs Cole, and he'd been through the game so many times in his head it was like he'd played 90 minutes twice over already. He hadn't thought that he'd also have to deal with the rest of the team.

'Why? What's he said?'

'Well, he's said nothing about it to us, has he? But then we're not his best mate, are we? Come on, you must know!'

Chris took a moment to think about what he was hearing. He decided to be cautious and wait.

'Why's Nicky leaving Spirebrook?' Griff asked impatiently, as if Chris had somehow managed to miss the question (as if!).

Chris felt a weight drop away from him. This wasn't about what had happened on the river bank! Could it really be that the others didn't know?

'Nicky's going to Bolton to live with his aunt and try and get into the Manchester United youth set-up,' he said hurriedly.

'Is that it?' cried Griff. Behind him, Fuller and Packham were exchanging 'told you so' glances. Clearly, the rumours were only just starting – no-one had the slightest idea of what was going on.

'That's all he's said to me,' Chris replied, which was certainly true.

'He's got that ten thousand quid,' said Fuller, who had been holding on to that theory for over a week now and wasn't about to let it go.

'Well,' said Griff. 'You lot will be in a right state next season, losing your best player.'

Hearing that from Griff, who wasn't a founder member of the Nicky Fiorentini fan club, hurt Chris.

'Nicky's not our best player,' he said sourly.

'No, I am,' said Griff, grinning, and thumping himself on the chest like a gorilla. 'And what with me and Fuller going up a grade and Nicky going to Manchester, you're just about stuffed for next season.'

Chris found himself laughing loudly along with the others. He didn't know why. 'How did practice go last night?' he asked.

'Brilliant!' jeered Fuller, beaming broadly. 'We're so sharp they should make us wear a sheath.'

Packham snorted, trying to cover his mouth with his hand, and Fuller turned to slap him around the head, demanding to know what he was sniggering at.

'Nicky was on top form,' Griff explained. 'He had us all running round like hares.' Chris could see that Griff hadn't liked Nicky stealing his authority, but there was no doubting the genuine admiration in his voice when he continued, 'And he played a blinder. No-one could get near him. And he was dropping passes on a five-pence coin.'

'If you've got your shooting boots on, the game's in the bag!' shouted Fuller, punching at the air.

Griff looked at his watch. 'The bus should be here by now. Come on, we'll go and find Flea. Put him out of his misery.'

They walked over towards the gym. Most of them had left their gear there already. Chris had his in his hand.

'Where's your bag?' asked Griff.

'In the wash,' remarked Chris, and he didn't bother to explain.

Most of the rest of them were already there, Nicky included. The team slowly gathered into a tight knot, each of them making sure the others were ready.

'I'm bricking myself,' Mac told Chris. 'Are you nervous?'

Suddenly, Chris realised what it was that was eating away at him inside. It wasn't the business with Nicky, not directly anyway. He wasn't nervous. There just weren't any butterflies in his stomach at all. Normally, he was as tight as a drum before the kick-off; now here he was, a few hours away from the most important game of his life, and he was totally unfocused.

Realising that made him feel almost afraid.

'This is stupid,' he told himself. 'I'm frightened because I'm not frightened enough.'

He dumped his bag on the ground. He and Nicky were separated by most of the rest of the group, but he could hear the other boy's voice, light and cheerful, laughing and joking with some of the others.

Flea appeared, trying to count heads. There were more than eleven kids and a few substitutes there, though, so he was reduced to calling out the team list as if it were a class register.

'MacIntyre, Brewster, Griffith, Packham, Jones, Javinder...' Some of the other kids started cheering each name as it was called, as if a Premiership team was being announced over the tannoy. One by one, the team dispersed, picking up their kit and heading for a coach parked at the side of the gym.

'... Fuller, Marsh ...'

Suddenly, Nicky was standing at Chris's side.

'You fit to play?' he asked, with no hint of emotion in his voice.

Instinctively, Chris touched the back of his head, then nodded.

'... Fiorentini ...'

Nicky grabbed Chris's bag. 'I'll put this on the coach for you,' he said, and set off towards the back where the driver was loading their kit.

'... Lucas ...'

Chris watched Nicky board the coach, having left their stuff with the driver. He knew that what had happened between them was neither forgotten nor forgiven, but maybe it could be set aside, just for today.

'... Stephens.'

That strange empty, gnawing feeling that had been scraping away at the back of Chris's mind didn't disappear as they made their way to the game. Worse than that, he felt a heavy cloud settle on him as the coach crawled through the city's afternoon traffic, rumbling over the bridge towards Star Park. Everyone was nervous, but Chris knew that this wasn't just a case of pre-match butterflies. Some of the others were trying to sing a rude song about a wandering fart; Chris couldn't even remember the words.

The coach crept slowly through the gates at Star Park and parked in front of the main entrance to the Easter Road Stand. Everyone was chattering noisily, looking around as they went through a door marked 'Club Entrance' and up to the directors' lounge.

It should have been the greatest day of Chris's life. Several of the Oldcester stars were there, along with the manager and some of the coaching staff. Both Ray Foulds and Sean Priest gave him the thumbs-up.

They met their opponents, and several dignitaries from the city, including the mayor. Everyone was on their best behaviour, including Baynham, who nibbled a few of the snacks on offer without clearing the table.

Finally, the two teams were taken down to the dressing rooms to get ready. By comparison with Old Trafford's, Oldcester's changing rooms were small and dark, but they could hear voices cheering from outside. East Sheils had brought a lot of support, and the boys hoped that Mrs Cole would change her mind about letting Spirebrook off early so they could get to the game too.

Chris took a seat close to the door. For the first time ever, he went through the ritual of getting changed without Nicky's excited chatter in his ear. The two Manchester United shirts were at the top of the bag, and Chris looked up, wondering if he should give Nicky his now. He decided against it and burrowed down to pull out his kit.

Twenty minutes later, with some last encouraging words from Flea in their ears, Spirebrook went out on to the pitch.

As he left the dressing room last, Chris rubbed his shirt badge. He ran up the tunnel and on to the pitch.

The cheer wasn't deafening but it put a real spring in their step. Maybe 200 kids from East Sheils were there, along with a hundred or so parents from the two schools, all clustered under the directors' box in the Easter Road Stand. The rest of the stadium was empty. It felt quite unnatural.

As he turned to face the spectators, Chris realised to his horror that he hadn't been last out on to the pitch. Nicky ran past him, without a glance or a word. He must have tucked himself out of sight in the dressing room at the last moment. Chris felt that terrible empty feeling inside once again. Nothing felt right about the situation at all.

The ref went over to have a few words. Mostly it was about enjoying the game, playing it cleanly and not arguing with decisions. Even though he couldn't have known Fuller, he addressed much of his speech at him. Knowing Fuller, he'd soon be telling everyone that the ref had been 'got at'.

'May the best team win,' said the ref.

'Yeah,' said Nicky. 'May the best man win.' He was looking Chris dead in the eye as he said it.

The tension was running higher now. Griff gathered the team around him in a huddle, as if they were an American football team. 'Listen to me, all of you,' he said, 'we're better than them, and this is our cup. Don't muck it up. I didn't come here to lose.'

That was all they got by way of a team talk from their captain, who wandered off to the centre circle for the coin toss. He wandered back a few moments later.

'We lost. They'll play from the north end first. We'll kick off.'

Chris couldn't help but wonder if it wasn't some kind of omen.

Fifteen

From beginning to end, the final was an unmitigated disaster for Spirebrook. Mac looked even smaller than usual in the vast goal, and East Sheils were tempted into striking from range from the first minute, just to test him out. The third shot went over Mac's head and into the top right corner, leaving him clawing at the empty air.

Fuller was acting like a maniac. From the kick-off, he raced around after the ball like a headless chicken. He fouled one of the East Sheils strikers, then whinged bitterly about an offside decision that wasn't given. The ref booked him. Five minutes later, he swore loudly after the ref gave a corner which Fuller insisted he hadn't touched, and he was sent off.

'I don't believe it!' cried Griff, throwing his hands in the air. East Sheils scored from the corner, a thumping, high header that Mac didn't get within two feet of. Twenty minutes gone, and Spirebrook were 2–0 behind, down to ten players and hopelessly dispirited.

Chris couldn't get himself into the game at all. It was like a waking dream, something he just floated around in the middle of, unable to alter anything, unable to influence the way Spirebrook were plummeting to defeat. His only achievements in the first half hour were to take three kick-offs and to miss a golden chance to put Phil Lucas through when he was completely unmarked. Chris just hadn't seen him.

Only one player was having a decent game for Spirebrook and that was Nicky. The East Sheils left back just wasn't good enough and Nicky was starting to torment him, just as he had made a fool of the Blackmoor defence in the quarter-final. One cross found Lucas at the back post, and the header went just over. Another excellent pass gave

Chris a run at the centre back, but he was beaten in the tackle.

Bit by bit, Nicky even started acting as captain, geeing up the other players and sorting out the hole in midfield left by Fuller's early bath. He tackled hard, covering the pitch from side to side. The East Sheils manager put one of their midfield players on to Nicky, telling him to mark him tightly. Nicky ran the poor guy all over the field, leaving him chasing shadows and gasping for air long before half-time.

This gave Javinder a little space, and Spirebrook started playing as if they were starting to believe in themselves again.

'Get a goal before half-time and we can still win this!' Flea called to Chris. The East Sheils fans were still cheering, but not with the same confidence as before.

Chris noticed that the crowd was swelling too, and that more and more blue jackets were becoming visible beside the deep green of East Sheils.

' "Andy" let them come early, after all,' said Griff, nodding at the growing band of Spirebrook fans. 'Come on, Chris — we can still do this!'

Chris tried to shake off the dark gloom that had been cloaking him all afternoon. He darted forward, looking for space every time Nicky had the ball. On a couple of occasions he was in the clear, but Nicky didn't see him. More often, Nicky's pass would be into space, asking for Chris to run on to it, something that they had practised and perfected over the years. Today, though, the passes were just that fraction too long or into just too tight a position.

The East Sheils centre backs were two broad lads who looked like twins, with cropped reddish hair and vivid, desperate eyes. They were having to play at the top of their game, but they were just about holding Chris at bay.

Just before the break, though, they both went after Chris at the same time, while he was angling a run wide of the box. Nicky's pass came in, flat, low and fast — too fast. Chris couldn't control it. Luckily, however, the rebound went straight to Phil Lucas, and he fired a shot past the East Sheils keeper. There was barely time to kick off before the ref blew for half-time.

Chris sat on the bench in the dressing room, breathing

hard. He drank deeply from a dilute orange drink and chewed slowly on a banana. The rest of the lads looked even more tired, but Lucas's late goal had put a bit of hope back into them.

'You have to support the front players,' Mr Lea was telling the others. 'I know it's hard without Fuller, but you have to get back and defend when they have possession. There's not enough bodies between ball and goal. Make your tackles count; then push up and release the ball to Jazz and Nicky. They can make the game turn round.' He turned to Nicky. 'You're playing a blinder. Keep it up. Sooner or later, you and Chris will click like normal, and we'll have won eight-two.'

Nicky grinned. 'We can't lose,' he replied.

Flea suggested a few more adjustments, and tried to get Griff to get involved in the game again. Slowly, all around him, Chris could feel the team picking itself up once more, starting to believe they could come back from behind. After all, they'd done it so many times before.

Just before they went back out, Chris collared Mr Lea. 'Could I have a word?'

Flea looked annoyed and impatient, and he was even less happy when Chris waited doggedly for the rest of the team to leave the room before he said anything. All the team.

'What is it, Chris? Are you OK?'

'I'm fine, sir, but I think Jonesy is getting pretty tired. It might be best to put Mike on in a bit, so –'

Flea looked at Chris in a way he'd never done before. It was a cool, hard stare without even a small fraction of Flea's normal docile friendliness in it. 'Leave the rest of the team to me, Chris. I'm the manager. You just start playing the way you can do, instead of leaving everything to Nicky, and we'll be fine.'

Chris stiffened. The gnawing feeling suddenly disappeared. Flea was as good as telling him that the reason they were losing was down to him, and he didn't like it.

'I'll just finish my drink, sir,' he said, allowing Flea to leave ahead of him. He stood alone in the dressing room for a few seconds, and then slammed his fist against one of the lockers.

'Fine. May the best man win.'

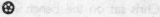

The second half almost started as badly as the first half had. East Sheils had taken off their exhausted midfield player during the break and replaced him with someone with fresh legs. Nicky was marked tight and the midfield was suddenly congested, with players from both sides playing a hard tackling game. Then Brewster miscued a clearance, which went straight to an East Sheils player.

Three-one. Once again, the Spirebrook players were left crestfallen. This time, though, Nicky wasn't able to rally them.

Nicky wasn't, but Chris was.

Nicky's passes were still fractionally off, but Chris was starting to anticipate them. He chased hard after everything, and the two red-headed defenders were put under enormous pressure. Chris's effort won Spirebrook a corner. Nicky floated it over, and even though it was a fraction too high, Chris got up and met it firmly. The keeper tipped it on to the bar.

Chris landed heavily. The impact helped him remember that he had promised his father that he wouldn't bang himself around. Still, Mrs Cole was going to make sure he had a long rest from school football after today, so what harm could one last game do?

He picked himself up and got stuck back into the game. Minutes later, he chased a ball Nicky had hit into the space behind the back four — over-hit, actually. The defender was always favourite to win the ball, but Chris slid in and took it off him cleanly. He pulled himself up, dragged the ball back with his heel, and was just looking around for someone to pass to when he was brought down from behind.

'Penalty!' yelled Lucas and about 200 other people. The ref called it a free kick, a yard outside the box. If Fuller hadn't already been sent off for shooting his mouth off, he would have gone then for sure. The red-headed defender looked as if he'd just been given an early Easter present.

Nicky bent the free kick over the wall, but too close to the keeper. Time was slipping away. Chris called Phil Lucas over.

'Tell Jazz to get another ball across to me like that one,' he said, breathing hard.

Phil nodded, his dark eyes sharp.

Chris didn't bother trying to repeat the message to Nicky.

93

Instead, he watched for Phil to give Jazz the message, and then motioned for Jazz to move wider.

The midfield battle was getting tougher. East Sheils was one of those schools that preferred rugby to football, and it was starting to show. Steve Jones took a whack on the shin and started hobbling. Flea took him off and put Mike Hurst on. Chris grinned to himself.

Twenty minutes left. Once again, Nicky was starting to get free. He almost managed to chip the keeper, and then he threaded a pass through to Lucas. Phil made a mess of collecting it, but bravely chased the ball towards the goal-line and won it back. The only pass he could make was a deep one back to Javinder.

Chris nodded at Jazz the moment he saw where the ball was going, and set off on a slicing run across the centre of the box. The pass came at him and hit first time, just a bit too high.

It was good enough, though. The big defenders were already rattled. One of them charged towards Chris as he stretched to gather the ball, slamming him to the ground.

The ref couldn't fail to give the penalty this time, although Griff did his best to make him change his mind by asking, 'Are you sure it's inside the box this time?'

Chris lay flat for a moment, aware of a sharp pain in his calf muscle. Moments later, Flea appeared with a wet sponge and a spray, looking the leg over as if he knew what he was doing. 'That'll bruise,' was his considered diagnosis. Chris sat up. 'You all right?'

'I think so. I'll try and run it off.' His leg felt stiff and sore. 'Get Nicky to take the penalty.'

Chris was the team's usual spot-kick expert, but Brewster sometimes had a whack if Chris wasn't able to. Flea opened his mouth as if to repeat his earlier instruction to Chris, then turned to Nicky and told him to take the kick.

Chris hobbled to the edge of the penalty area, then turned to watch Nicky take the kick. He wasn't sure what he was expecting. Nicky took a short run up and slotted the ball to the keeper's left without any fuss or bother. Chris couldn't help but grin.

He limped back towards the centre line. Flea observed him

from the side, anxiously watching for a sign as to whether he could continue.

'Are you going to be able to finish the game?' he called.

'No trouble.'

Although he didn't mean to, he looked up into the crowd and saw his father standing on the fringe of the knot of Spirebrook blue. He looked pretty stern. Well, it's not like I got hurt heading the ball, Chris said to himself.

The knock niggled at him, making it hard to break into a run. Perhaps, he thought, it would be best if he went off. He was still making up his mind when Marsh collided with one of East Sheils' midfield players, and they were both helped from the field.

That settled that. He'd have to try and tough it out. Gritting his teeth, Chris clapped his hands and tried to urge Spirebrook on once more.

East Sheils were watching Nicky very closely. Two black and white striped shirts were always in close attendance. But in closing down that option, they had left themselves open on the other flank. Javinder and Phil Lucas were playing some brilliant stuff. The 'twins' were having a rough time and the East Sheils manager was waving the midfield and forward players back so that they could defend in depth.

'They're bricking themselves,' puffed Griff, hauling Chris to his feet after another hard tackle.

Chris winced as he put his weight on his weaker leg.

'I'm glad. I don't want to face them when they feel mean.'

Another corner. This time, Brewster went over to take it so that he could swing in one of his fast, brutal specials. Chris went to the back post.

The ball flew over, skimming the head of the players at the near post and evading the keeper's outstretched gloves. Someone got a little touch on it, deflecting the ball down and slightly away from the goal, directly into Chris's path.

The ball was absolutely gagging to be volleyed back. Chris didn't have to stretch or do any more than turn his body and unleash his right foot. The impact jarred his injured leg, but he gave it absolutely everything.

It fairly screamed towards the top right-angle of the goal, and no-one seemed remotely interested in putting their bodies into its path. Except one person. Springing like a jack-in-the-box, Nicky suddenly appeared above the mass of ducking heads, planting his head in the trajectory of the ball. It hit him with a loud Bop!, almost snapping his head back and dropping him to the floor as if he'd been hit by a plank of wood.

The ball turned almost 90 degrees and bulged the back of the net out half a metre. A howl of amazement, triumph and pain echoed around the almost empty stadium.

Nicky was almost dazed by the hit he had taken (and it can't have helped that Griff and three of the others had jumped on him in celebration). He accepted Chris's out-stretched hand without realising who it was. Chris hauled him to his feet.

They jogged back to their own half, Chris still limping and Nicky shaking his head clear. Chris was laughing inside. If he was right, and Nicky had been deliberately selling Chris short to make him look bad — even if it meant losing the game — then his instincts had got the better of him. He just hadn't been able to resist sticking his head in the way of Chris's shot. Chris wondered if he should explain the symptoms of con-cussion to Nicky.

Instead, it was Nicky who managed to speak first.

'That's paid you back for one of the things I owe you for,' said Nicky. From a distance, it would look as if he was smiling, but Chris could see the delight was shallow and brittle.

'Really?'

'You stole a goal from me; now I've taken one from you.'

Chris felt his temper boiling inside. 'Is that what you've been doing? Letting the team lose just because of what's happened between us?' He knew that Nicky had been playing brilliantly for much of the game and that everyone would think he'd given it his best shot. Only Chris would ever realise that Nicky's best moments had all come when the team was two goals down.

'It's not my team any more,' said Nicky, spitefully.

They reached the halfway line. Nicky stayed wide; Chris started to move inside to cover the kick-off.

'You think you're so smart, Fiorentini.' He'd never used Nicky's surname on its own before. 'Well, you've managed to get it all wrong, as usual. That shot was probably going over before you "stole" it. And I saw through your plan – why do you think I got Flea to tell you to take the penalty? I knew you wouldn't miss on purpose, and let yourself look bad.' He broke into a run, widening the gap between them. 'Three-three, Nicky,' he called, knowing everyone could hear. 'We can still win!'

Ninety minutes came and went. So did extra time. East Sheils might have shot their bolt as far as winning the game went in regular play, but they could still defend in depth. Nicky faded from the game and Chris couldn't shake off the lasting grip of the whack on his leg. No-one else was able to spark Spirebrook into one last effort. They could have played for another hour and it would still have been a draw.

So, it would be penalties again. No-one wanted to see the County Schools Cup Final settled that way, but those were the rules.

The two teams collapsed in two small clumps in the centre circle, completely weary. At first they sat all mixed together, making several gallons of liquid disappear while the ref consulted with the two managers. Finally, Flea and the other manager came over to join them, sitting in the middle of the bunch. The two teams gradually separated.

'OK, I have to give the ref our first five names. Who's up for this? "Bruce", are you game?'

Brewster nodded, even though he looked very unhappy with the idea. The group suddenly took on the look of a line of kids waiting to get shots from some visiting nurse, or a biology class with a dissection lesson in front of it. No-one wanted to make eye contact with Flea; everyone wanted him to pick somebody else.

'I'll take one!' said Fuller, who had once volunteered to bite the specimen open when they couldn't find the scalpels in biology.

'You were sent off; you're not allowed to take a kick,' explained Flea. 'How about you, Phil? Yes? Jazz?' Three down. Chris waited to get the call. Flea kept looking around the ring of faces. 'Nicky? Fancy another one?'

Nicky shot a fierce glance in Chris's direction. 'Sure,' he said.

Flea finally turned to Chris. 'How's the leg?'

'I can manage.'

Flea considered this carefully. Finally, he nodded. 'I'll leave you to last. If we get lucky, we won't need you.'

'Yeah,' said Griff. 'If Brewster hits one of his specials up the middle, they might not have a goalkeeper to stop you anyway!'

Everyone laughed, Chris included. He wasn't nervous about taking the responsibility but he knew his leg was tightening up with every second. Perhaps it would be best if he didn't have to take one at all.

Spirebrook's players had divided into two types now. Those who didn't have to take a kick were looking almost relaxed; finishing their drinks, sitting back propped on their elbows. Those who did were looking pale and sickly, as if all the liquid in the world wouldn't have wet their throats.

Actually, there was a third type. Mac. The one person who didn't get asked if he wanted to be part of the shoot-out.

And he turned out to be the first of Spirebrook's participants. East Sheils would take the first kick. Mac made his way to the goal, getting smaller and smaller as the distance increased.

'I hate these . . .' muttered Griff, turning away.

The shoot-out began. Mac was beaten comprehensively four times. After the fourth, he was shaking with frustration.

'I *hate* being a goalkeeper!' he raged.

Meanwhile, Brewster had failed to win the game at the first attempt by blasting his kick wide of the Sheils keeper when Spirebrook had been hoping he would end up being strained through the net.

Phil hit one up the middle, right through where the keeper had been standing before he dived; Jazz sent him the wrong way. The Spirebrook supporters cheered, but too soon. The ref announced that he hadn't blown his whistle and Jazz would have to take the kick again.

It was so unfair. Fuller raged and Flea ran over to protest. The decision stood. Jazz had to retake, and this time – of course – the keeper turned it round the post.

'Come *on*, Nicky!' yelled Fuller. More and more people were looking away. Even on the Easter Road Stand they were starting to turn their backs before each kick. The tension was unbearable.

Chris had to watch Nicky's kick. If he missed, that would be that. In one moment, Nicky would have his revenge on team mates who didn't even know that he now despised them. Chris convinced himself that this was just what would happen.

Nicky scored.

On the way back, he spoke to Mac as they passed. He sat down in the centre circle without looking at anyone. Congratulations washed over him but he kept his eyes fixed on the goal.

Four-three. One kick left each. Now Mac was in the hot seat. The East Sheils player placed the ball, and lined up.

'He'll go left,' said Nicky quietly.

Mac took off the moment the ball was struck, and flew across the goal so far he almost hit the post as he landed. On the way, the ball chunked into his hands and stuck there.

There were screams from the stand. The East Sheils players dropped their heads into their hands.

'Told you . . .' said Nicky, and now he did look up, and he was smiling at Chris. It was the most human smile Chris had seen on his face for weeks. Nicky was *loving* this. Because he knew . . . he *knew* . . .

Chris went forward to take the last regular kick. Walking was murder. His leg was tightening up with every step, sending spears of pain up from his calf.

He placed the ball and turned back. This would have to be a short run up. Place the ball, he told himself. Keep it low, and just inside the post.

The silence all around him was like winter. He turned to face the goal, turning his shoulders to try and loosen the tension. He let the keeper see him look right with just a little flicker of the eyes.

Three short steps and he arrived over the ball, aiming low, aiming left. He could sense the keeper already starting to move the wrong way. He swung his right leg back and prepared to level the score.

And then his left foot twisted as he planted it, and his knee buckled, ever so slightly.

The penalty skewed off to the left. Chris could almost ignore the pain from his battered leg as he tried to will the ball back on course. But it was well wide, and the East Sheils supporters were already screaming in triumph as the ball knocked over one of the advertising boards, and disappeared.

The dressing room was a scene of complete dejection. From next door, loud singing and cheering drifted in, booming louder whenever one of the intervening doors opened. For Chris and his team mates, there were only a few consoling words from Flea and Mrs Cole (she'd arrived just in time to witness the disaster), and the hissing sound as some cans of coke were opened. Otherwise, they sat in silence. They had an invitation to go and join the winners upstairs for the presentation; there was food laid on and medals for all the losing team.

They changed slowly, with barely a word spoken between them. A few people had come up to say 'tough luck' to Chris. After a while, he started to feel like it was all his fault, even though he knew it wasn't true.

'Chris?'

The voice belonged to Ray Foulds. He and Sean Priest had come in to compliment the team on a game well played.

'How's the leg?' asked Priest.

'It'll be OK.' Chris showed them the bruise, which was developing in that sickly yellow-purple colour that showed it would be a really ugly mark for days.

'Turn up next Wednesday even if it's not a hundred per cent,' Priest said. 'You can meet everyone and take a look around. Riverside could do with a player like you.'

Chris looked round quickly. That was the kind of thing he didn't want Nicky to hear. Fortunately (but strangely), Nicky was nowhere in sight.

'Not your day,' said Foulds. 'Maybe that bang on the head hasn't gone away just yet.'

'I thought I played OK,' said Chris. 'Second half, at least.'

100

'You did,' said Foulds. 'That isn't what I meant.'

'Shame about Nicky going up north,' Priest continued. 'The Colts wouldn't say no to him either.'

Chris looked up. 'Then why didn't you ask him to come along last week?'

Priest glanced quickly at Foulds. 'I made a mistake about Nicky. I didn't think he was that good at the trials — too self-centred, too flash. I was wrong, though, and you two were right. He's quite a player.'

'You couldn't tell him all that, could you?' asked Chris.

'I'd be glad to. Where is he?'

They all looked around. Flea, who was on the fringe of the conversation, stepped forward.

'Nicky? He's just leaving. His uncle came to pick him up — he arrived just before the end. They're going up to Manchester tomorrow, apparently . . .'

Chris wasn't listening. He'd leapt to his feet and grabbed at his bag, trying to pull the two shirts from inside. The bag split right open, as if it had been sliced in two, and the shirts spilled out with everything else.

'Nicky!' yelled Chris, grabbing at the Giggs shirt. He was racing to the door when he heard Flea shout his name.

He turned. Flea was bending, picking something up from the floor, something that had spilled from Chris's bag with the rest of the stuff. A small white box, with something inside rattling. Most of the writing on the box was tiny, but there were a few words in large black print. A brand name, and the words 'ANABOLIC STEROID'.

Chris gaped at the box, at Flea, at Sean Priest, and at all the other faces, which were just on the turn from surprise to horror. A jumble of words started to tumble from his brain, but only one managed to get as far as his mouth.

'NICKY!!!!!'

Part 2
6 months later

Sixteen

Chris hit the ball and it whistled over the wall in a graceful arc, into the goal past the diving keeper's outstretched hands.

'Not again!' howled Mac. 'I hate it when you do that!'

Chris laughed, and waited for the ball to be thrown back. Mac took his time about it.

'You were begging for trouble, standing that close to the far post. All I had to do was chip the ball over the wall and you were going to have a really hard time getting to it.'

'I have to stand pretty wide or I can't see you!'

That was the problem in using a fence to stand in for a defensive wall — the spaces between the slats were just too small. The trouble for Mac was that he suffered the same problem with a wall of players. He was just too short to be able to see over it.

'Try it again,' said Chris.

They lined up as they had before, with Mac patrolling the 'goal' (two kit bags with their jackets draped over them). Chris saw that he had moved much closer to the near post this time.

He changed the angle of his run up slightly and struck the outside of the ball with his instep. The spinning ball started to curve almost as soon as it left his boot, this time bending around the end of the fence to land a foot inside the far post. Mac hadn't even moved.

'Oh, very funny,' he moaned.

A car horn sounded a short, sharp 'parp', and the boys turned to see a dark grey saloon gliding over the car park's gravel, pulling up outside the clubhouse. After a moment, the door opened and Sean Priest stepped out.

'You two are here first then,' he called.

'As usual!' shouted Chris, beaming.

Priest went round to the back of the car to fetch his gear from the boot. He dropped his bag on the step as he walked by, and went over to where Chris and Mac were practising.

'It only takes a couple of minutes to get here from school now they've opened up the old lane,' Chris remarked.

Priest nodded and inspected their practice set-up, lined up round the corner of the fence around the tennis courts.

'What's this?'

'We've been working on free kicks, after what happened against Argyle Street last Sunday. Mac's having trouble seeing the ball until it's gone past the wall.'

Priest nodded again, his face lined in thought. 'Take another one for me, will you Chris?'

He crouched on his haunches while Chris and Mac went through the drill again. This time, Chris bent the ball off the outside of his boot, dropping it over the wall. Mac scrambled to get over to it, just managing to fumble it away.

Priest stood up and scratched his beard. 'It's just as well there aren't too many players in the League who can bend a ball as well as you can, Chris. But you're right. We'll have to work on defending against free kicks and see if we can't get Mac some support.'

'What I want is for you to find someone else to be in goal,' moaned Mac.

Priest smiled. This was a familiar argument.

'We're looking, Mac — honest we are. But, like it or not, you're actually pretty good, and I'm not ready to give up on you just yet!'

Others were starting to arrive, dropped off by parents or walking from the bus stop on the main road. Soon, quite a noisy throng was gathered outside the clubhouse, waiting for Priest to unlock the doors.

It was a warm, breezy September evening, early in the new year at Spirebrook and a new football season for Riverside Colts. They'd played their first game of the new campaign only the weekend before, and drawn 1–1. Chris had scored the Colts' goal with a long-range shot.

'Right!' called Priest, clapping his hands together to get their attention. 'Tonight I want to work on some set pieces, particularly free kicks. I'm not happy with the way the wall is being placed or with the way Mac is getting too little a sight of the ball. So, what we're going to work on is this . . .'

Chris half-listened as Priest outlined his ideas. In the few months since he had joined the Colts, Chris had come to respect him enormously. Technically, the Colts' manager was Iain Walsh but it was a well-known 'secret' that Priest kept a very close eye on Riverside, looking for players who could step up to become part of Oldcester United's youth scheme once they were a bit older.

Because they recruited some of the best players from the western edges of Oldcester, Riverside were strong contenders to win the Oldcester and County Youth League almost every year. This year, people were saying, they stood a very good chance of doing the double, with both the Under-14s and the Under-16s teams.

An away draw in their first game was slightly disappointing, but they had played some superb football and Chris had felt immediately at home, even though it was his first competitive game with the side. Over the summer, he had trained with the Colts twice a week, and had slotted into the side as if he was a five-year veteran.

The highlight had been a three-day visit to Holland, to play against youth teams from Ajax, PSV and Rotterdam — the latter being the club where Priest had finished his career.

Ajax had given the Colts a walloping, but they'd beaten PSV and Rotterdam and the trip had taught them a lot about their strengths and weaknesses. Ajax in particular had made them look very slow and clumsy on the ball. The whole team had returned to England determined to sharpen up their game in every department.

It had been one of the best summers of Chris's life.

And to think he had almost missed out on it all.

It was hard to remember every detail of that horrible moment in the dressing room after the county final, but Chris knew his whole footballing life had been on the line for a while. Everyone had taken a good look at that box and asked Chris where it had come from. They wanted to know if he understood how dangerous steroids were. Priest told him flatly that if he thought Chris would play around with stuff like that, then he'd never play for Oldcester, Riverside or any other club he had any influence over.

Chris had denied all knowledge of the box and its contents, of course, but it had been a long while before he knew that he had earned their trust again. A friend of Flea's who worked in a chemist's shop finally settled the argument — the tablets weren't steroids, they were asthma pills.

Although Chris couldn't provide a satisfactory answer as to why the pills were in his bag, except to say that it wasn't his usual kit bag and maybe they'd been in there when he'd packed it, the crisis was over. He was given a stern warning that people would keep an eye on him, but that was all.

He'd turned up with his father at Riverside the week after and had a long talk with Sean Priest. The incident was put behind them. No-one would bring it up again.

Chris thought about it every now and again, but it looked like one of those mysteries that wouldn't ever be solved. Slowly, the worst parts of the memory slipped from his mind.

Chris concentrated instead on Riverside Colts and on getting himself back into Mrs Cole's good books by working hard throughout the summer term. 'Andy' wasn't the sort of head teacher who changed her mind about punishments, but three weeks before the end of the year, she did tell Chris that the ban would be lifted when they came back in September. They had just started the second week back, and Flea was rebuilding the team that had lost the final and which was now short of a serious number of senior players, with Griff, Fuller, Marsh and Nicky among those who had moved up a grade or moved away completely.

It would be good to pull on Spirebrook's blue shirt again and to set about wiping away the memories of that horrible day. Tonight, though, it was the blue and white of Riverside Colts.

'Isn't that right, Chris?'

Priest's voice pierced Chris's daydream, and he looked around, immediately aware that everyone was looking at him.

'You're always right, boss,' he said, grinning, and everyone jeered.

'Is the correct answer!' Priest shouted over the din, just as if he was a game show host with a rowdy audience. 'Now wake up, dozy!'

He threw a piece of chalk at Chris, who headed it out through the door. The cheering grew even louder. Practice with the Colts was always harder on the eardrums than it was on any muscle in the body.

It was almost quieter to be at Star Park. Life in the Endsleigh League after four seasons in the top flight was a lot less hectic, and the crowds were much smaller than they had been for the Premiership.

During the closed season, United had had to sell three of their top players as well, and there were rumours that the manager and several others in the back room would be sacked if the results weren't good immediately the new season started.

'Not quite the same as the European Championship, is it?' Chris's father said as they settled into their seats in the half-empty stadium.

'No, this is better,' said Chris. After England had been knocked out, the European Championship had seemed to lose a lot of its interest, although there was a lot to admire in the way Spain and Germany played on their way to the final. Chris had supported Spain – after all, they did play in red and blue – and it had been good to see them win.

But Chris couldn't get interested in international football. It was never the same team twice, and the manager always seemed to ignore anyone who was any good. No, Chris thought, give me League football any day. Of course, he would have been happier if Oldcester were still playing Arsenal, Blackburn and Newcastle rather than Leicester, Derby and Sheffield United, but you can't have everything –

'Do you hear from Pete Baynham at all?' Chris's father asked.

'No, not a lot. He phoned just after his dad got back from Bosnia; do you remember?'

Chris's father nodded and opened his programme to see who Norwich were fielding against United that afternoon. Then he checked his watch.

'They're late coming out,' he said.

Just at that moment, the tannoy announced that there was a problem getting the away supporters into the ground. The crowd jeered. Holding up the game because 40 Norwich supporters had left it to the last minute to arrive wasn't anyone's idea of fun. 'Nothing from Nicky, either?'

Chris avoided looking at his dad. He was sure everyone knew something about what had happened, but he'd always kept the whole story to himself. As far as his father knew, he and Nicky had parted as friends.

'Too busy, I expect. They work them hard at Old Trafford.'

'Sure.' Another few moments passed. Chris started to get a nagging feeling that this conversation had a point to it somewhere. 'You don't wish you'd gone, do you?'

'Where?' asked Chris, trying hard to keep up with his father's wandering mind.

'Old Trafford. Do you wish you'd gone with Nicky?'

'What, and leave you in that house on your own?'

His father laughed. 'Are you worried that I'd have wild parties every night?'

'That's what I do when you're not there,' Chris replied.

They laughed together for a moment.

'No, I mean it. Suppose we could have worked something out ... would you have wanted to try your luck up there? You're good enough, you know, to play for United. In a few years' time –'

'No, I didn't want to go,' Chris interrupted him, and it almost surprised him just how sure he was of that. 'Do you think I could ever have given up coming here and seeing a proper game of football?'

The crowd were getting restless. Over at the south end, a small group of yellow-clad supporters were slipping sheepishly into the stand. Twelve thousand other supporters booed them in welcome.

'Listen,' said Chris's dad, his face suddenly quite serious. 'I've got something I need to tell you; something we have to talk about. The company are going to get rid of some people. I could take redundancy and we could move somewhere else; start fresh. It doesn't have to be Manchester. In fact, if I stay with the firm, they want me to move to their new office in Scotland –'

'Scotland?!' cried Chris.

'That's what they said. So, what I'm saying is, we can either go to Scotland or I can take redundancy and we can move somewhere else. Or we could stay here and see what happens.'

Chris watched his father's face carefully, looking for a sign as to how he felt about all this. To Chris, it was all so unreal. Scotland, moving, new jobs, new homes? What was he supposed to think?

'What do you want to do?'

'I don't know ... that's why I thought we ought to talk about it.'

Chris tried to think. Now that he'd got himself sorted at school and Riverside and everything, did he really want to see all that go away?

'Suppose United go straight back up,' he said, 'and we miss it. How would that feel? I don't think I could cope –'

'You reckon we'll go back up?'

'Easy! We'll beat this lot for a start ...'

Chris's father paused, thinking about what his son had just said. Chris watched him reach a decision.

'OK. Here's the deal. If we win today, we stay. If we lose, I'll take the redundancy and we'll try our luck somewhere else.'

There was a brief moment when Chris thought that this was a rather risky way of planning your future. But then he thought, Why not?

'What if it's a draw?'

'Scotland?'

'I don't think so. We'll have to have a replay.'

'OK – oh, here they come at last.'

The two teams jogged out on to the pitch to the ironic cheers of the impatient supporters. The tannoy started to list the eight or nine changes to the published programme ...

'What *are* they wearing?' Chris's father laughed.

Chris looked up from the team lists. 'That's their away strip.'

'Away strip? Away strip? What do they need with an away strip? Who else plays in canary yellow?'

Chris chuckled. It certainly was very hard on the eyes out there, what with the bright green of the grass, the sharp red

111

and blue of United's kit, and now City's dazzling riot of lime-green and white.

'Our lads will need sunglasses,' his father complained.

Chris settled back to enjoy the game. Somehow, he had a good feeling about this afternoon and United's chances. Whatever else happened, Chris couldn't ever imagine moving away from Oldcester or following a team who could change colours as often as some of them did.

'Come on United!!!' he yelled, and he spent the next 90 minutes supporting them like never before.

As they left the stadium, a light drizzle was falling. Nothing, though, could dampen the way Chris was feeling. They'd asked the game to send them a sign, and it did. A walloping sign.

'Mark Fisher's never scored a hat-trick before,' Chris reminded his father. Funnily enough, he'd been reading that fact in the club yearbook only the night before.

'Ten goals all last season,' his father agreed.

'I guess we'll be staying, then.'

'Looks like it.'

They followed the cheering throng through the gates. Chris stayed close behind a man listening to the final scores on his radio, relaying the scores to everyone around them.

'Manchester United won . . .'

'They'll be tough to beat this year,' Chris's father commented, and several other people around nodded in agreement. Then Chris noticed his dad was staring off into the distance ahead, as if he had recognised someone.

'Look, there's Nicky's uncle. What's his name — Fabio?'

'Fabian,' corrected Chris, flatly.

'No sign of Nicky . . . I don't suppose he gets home much.'

'I don't think he does,' said Chris. His father was still looking up ahead. Chris couldn't see over the heads of the crowd, but he imagined Fabian Fiorentini must be standing on the corner, outside the newsagents. He was still trying to think of an excuse as to why they should head the other way when he realised they'd been spotted.

'Hey! Hello!' Chris recognised Uncle Fabian's cheerful voice at once. He was surprised to hear it sounding so welcoming – he'd assumed he was probably in the bad books of the entire Fiorentini family. 'Mr Stephens . . . it's good to see you. Quite a match today, eh?'

'It certainly was. Chris and I were talking earlier about whether United will go back up straight away –'

'I'm sure of it!' said Uncle Fabian (Chris made a mental note to himself to stop calling him that). 'Chris – it's good to see you! How's the old school, then?'

Chris answered cautiously. Unc– Fabian seemed quite genuinely pleased to see him, but that was so far away from what Chris had expected that he felt quite nervous.

'Pretty good . . .'

'Have you started the new season, yet?'

'Not properly, no. The first game's in a couple of weeks.'

'That Mr Lea, he should get the teams together at the end of the summer vacation, not leave it until the term starts. It always takes so long to get everything going at the beginning of the year.'

'I expect you're right,' said Chris.

There was an awkward silence. Clearly, both the adults were waiting for Chris to ask a particular question, one which Chris wasn't sure he wanted to ask. He really did feel very confused in this situation.

'How's Nicky doing?' asked his father, clearly tired of waiting.

'Really good!' said Fabian (which sounded just as unnatural to Chris's mind; perhaps he should try Mr Fiorentini?). 'Apparently, the new school is a bit of a shock. It's a very select school and they aren't so easy on the boys as at Spirebrook, eh?' He laughed and ruffled Chris's hair, which was something Chris absolutely hated. 'But he's really enjoying training with Manchester United.' Mr Fiorentini continued, puffing himself up proudly. 'You should see the facilities they have up there, Chris.'

'I did,' Chris reminded him. Mr Fiorentini halted abruptly, his dark eyebrows sloping deeply as he frowned. Chris's father nudged him in the back. 'You're right,' Chris added, grudgingly. 'It's a brilliant set-up.'

Uncle Fabian (Chris faced facts, that was the only way he

could think of him) was smiling again, his bushy black moustache arched up over his bright lips and white teeth.

'I bet you miss him a lot, eh? It's a pity you two have split up. Still, it's not like he's vanished from the face of the earth, eh? He'll be home most weekends, and at half-term. You could come over –'

'Yeah, maybe,' said Chris coughing.

'Perhaps I'd better get you home,' said his father, and he turned to stretch his hand out to Nicky's uncle. 'It was good to see you again.'

'The same for me, Mr Stephens.'

'Please, call me John.'

'OK. John. I'm Fabian. Everyone in our family calls me Uncle Fabian, but for you, I'll make an exception.'

The two men laughed and shook hands warmly.

'Think you'll be over here much this season?' asked Chris's father.

'Sure, yes. I'm using the season ticket we had for Nicky. Perhaps I should sit with you, eh?' He laughed again, louder than ever.

'Just don't expect me to buy you hot dogs,' said Chris's father, and the two men shook hands again.

They were still laughing as they separated. Chris said goodbye in the lowest voice he could manage.

'What a lunatic,' said his father, shaking his head. 'The whole family is completely barking, you know.'

'I know.'

'It's good that Nicky is doing so well, isn't it? And you two should be able to keep in touch after all.'

'Great!' said Chris, with all the enthusiasm he could fake.

Suddenly, Scotland didn't look so bad an option after all.

Seventeen

It started to look as though Griff was going to be proved right. Chris's team at Spirebrook didn't look anything like as strong as last year's. Of course, Griff wasn't crowing about it too much, because now that he'd moved up an age bracket, he was finding it hard to get into the school team. Fuller wasn't playing at all.

Three weeks into the new term, Flea called Chris in to see him. 'How do you feel about becoming captain?' he asked.

Frankly, Chris was amazed. Even though the business over those pills had been cleared up, Flea had never shown much sign of trusting Chris as he had trusted Griff. The fact was — and just about everyone knew this — Flea had wanted Nicky to be captain after Griff moved up, and he was disappointed to have lost him.

'I'd be happy to be captain,' Chris told him.

Flea nodded thoughtfully. He was drinking tea from a plastic mug, the same mug he had used when he had been chatting with Foulds about pairs of players, like those two West Ham strikers.

'You don't sound very enthusiastic,' he said.

'I'm just surprised, that's all. I thought you might pick Bruise, or maybe Mike Hurst. You normally pick a defender –'

'When I picked Griff, everyone said I normally picked midfielders.'

Chris laughed — he was sure the story was true. Flea always seemed to be arguing with other teachers and parents because he didn't behave the way they expected. Even his nickname gave people a false impression. Brand-new first years told to go and look for a teacher called 'Flea' didn't expect to find themselves faced with a 6' 4" ex-prop forward with a head that looked as though it was carved from granite.

'What about your commitments with Riverside?'

'They won't get in the way. In fact, I think they'll help. I'm learning an awful lot with them.'

'Good. We need a few new ideas. We're going to be a bit short of experience in defence this year. I'd like to think that you and Phil will still be able to do good work up front, even without Nicky.'

'We'll give it our best shot,' said Chris.

'Good. OK, well, I'll tell everyone at practice next week. Our first League game is on Thursday, remember. A friend of mine tells me that Blackmoor are looking for revenge after last year.'

'They can dream,' said Chris, standing up to go.

Flea was staring off into space, the mug of tea dangling precariously in his hand. 'That goal you scored,' he said, 'was one of the best I've ever seen.'

Chris almost blushed. 'Thank y–' he started to say.

'That cross Nicky laid through was absolutely on the money, wasn't it? Even Fuller could have put that away. Absolute magic.'

Chris sighed, and left Flea reminiscing about the quarter-final. The bright sun outside the gym made him blink, and he took a moment to get used to the light and to clear his thoughts.

'Fuller would still have been on the halfway line wondering what to do next . . .' he muttered to himself, then he told himself off for being spiteful about the wrong target, and set off for double maths.

It wasn't easy concentrating on school work (or anything else!) during the first weeks of term. Nicky's dark shadow seemed to fall on everything Chris did.

For a start, the contractors had finally moved in with a vengeance on the old chemical works. The last few buildings had disappeared back in May and the lane had been converted into an access road, linking the new shopping complex with the High Street and the road which ran from the university into Spirebrook. The new superstore had already opened, but they were still building more warehouses and showrooms all over the area where Chris had chased Nicky. Twenty-odd years of delay had been overtaken by a frenzy of industry, almost as if everyone was frightened that if things weren't built quickly, they'd have to stop altogether.

Mrs Cole was even talking about changing the regulations once the building work was finished.

Just about all that was left was the old bridge, which had been given a fresh coat of green paint and was supposedly going to carry a light railway in from the suburbs and on through to the city centre. The walkway along the river had been tidied up and seats and litter-baskets and flowerpots had been added, so that people could enjoy a scenic walk along the river.

Chris had been along there just once. When he reached the bridge, he saw that a bright neon light had been added.

Every day, the distant clattering of JCBs and heavy earth-movers rattled the school windows and reminded Chris of that fateful day. There was even a dredger in the river, clearing out all the muck so that the fish might return. Chris wondered if they'd find his bag down there, along with all the shopping trolleys and discarded mattresses.

He thought about Nicky every time he went to Star Park. The seat next to him was now occupied by a sixteen-year-old girl who came with her boyfriend. She kept screaming at all the wrong moments.

Naturally, Nicky's ghost haunted the dressing room in the school gym, and Chris couldn't go past the gaunt, grey pylons without remembering the competition they had had during their first week together. And Nicky's influence was missing in the team, no doubt about it. They didn't have the same creative spark at all any more.

Wherever he went and whatever he did, Chris kept banging into reminders of stuff he and Nicky had got up to, and places where they had hung out together. It was good remembering some of the things they'd done.

But if anyone asked Chris if he was missing Nicky, Chris was always able to answer the same way: 'No'. And it was the truth. He had left Nicky in the past, like some old shirt that no longer fitted properly. Because Chris knew . . . he *knew* . . .

117

Nicky had been the one at fault. Nicky had been the one so desperate to impress Foulds and Priest and all the people at Old Trafford that he had been jealous of any attention coming Chris's way. And, Chris was sure, Nicky had done everything he could to make Spirebrook lose the county final, short of scoring five own goals and missing the penalty.

Finally – and this was what hurt the most – Chris suspected that there was only one way those pills could have found their way into his bag. Nicky had taken the bag off him when they got on the bus. It had to have been then. It had to have been Nicky.

Chris had thought about it over and over again, and although he couldn't quite make all the pieces fit properly, he knew that Nicky had gone from being his best friend to his worst enemy in those few short weeks the previous spring. Any time Chris thought he might be wrong, he only had to remember going under that bridge. He could feel Nicky crashing into him, and the stunning impact as he'd hit the bollard that had saved him from falling into the river.

There was only one place where Chris didn't think about Nicky, and that was at the university sports ground, where the Colts practised and played their home games. That was all Chris's, and it was the one place he could go to and feel completely free.

Rory Blackstone, a big-boned Irish lad, played alongside Chris up front. Rory was the target man, the sort of player who was most comfortable getting the ball with his back to goal; a sort of ginger-headed Mark Hughes. He could either lay it off, or turn with surprising speed and aim for goal.

Defenders hated him, and they tried to make sure he was always crowded for space. Consequently, Chris seemed to find all the room in the world.

Iain Walsh, who played in the Riverside senior team and ran the youth team, had encouraged Chris to find even more space by playing a little wider. This allowed him to make darting runs into the box, looking for little lay-offs from Rory or taking the ball in himself. Chris was hitting the ball harder than ever; bending it either way in the air. And he was heading the ball well too. He was looking forward to the new season enormously. The way he figured it, it had to be an improvement on the one before.

The Eastbury defenders had pushed up and were all raising their arms for offside as Chris pounced through a small gap, taking the pass from Javinder and sprinting towards the goal.

That was exactly the same trick Eastbury Comprehensive had pulled on Spirebrook every time Chris had played them. Quite a few of the lads from the comp played in Eastbury Town's youth team, including the huge kid with black hair who had swamped Chris in his first year. Chris was too quick for him now, and he'd caught up a lot in height.

Eastbury were the sort of team who stuck to something that worked for them, even when it stopped working. Chris had already sprung the offside trap twice that afternoon.

The goalkeeper came out to narrow the angle. Chris took the ball directly at him, then feinted to shoot. As he spread himself, Chris flicked the ball to one side and then hit it over the falling keeper in the next stride. The ball bounced twice into the empty net.

'That's better, Riverside!' yelled Priest from the touchline. 'Ten more minutes now!'

Eastbury weren't going to come back from 4–1 down, so that was that. The final whistle blew.

Chris leapt up and punched the air in delight, cracked hands with his team mates, and then shook hands with the unhappy defenders as they trooped from the ground. The big black-haired defender looked at him closely, scratching his head and squinting his eyes tight as if Chris was a ghost or some mirage that he couldn't quite make out.

'I know you, don't I?' said the lad.

'I play for Spirebrook Comp as well,' said Chris.

'Oh, right – you've got that flash winger with the big mouth.' Chris couldn't believe it – this was the place he came to get away from Nicky-flamin'-Fiorentini! He was about to say something when the other lad added, 'Looks like you don't need him with this lot, though. You did us easy today. Well played.'

Chris returned the compliment and ran off the pitch,

feeling even better. Two goals, a comfortable win, and the respect of a player who used to make him feel about two feet tall.

'Good one, Chris,' said Priest as he went off.

Iain Walsh slapped him on the back.

'I'm glad you talked me into giving Javinder a run,' said the Colts' manager. 'He's all right, isn't he?'

'Three or four of those passes . . .' Chris replied, a little short of breath, 'and it was just like –'

He halted. Had he really been going to say what he thought he'd been going to say? Priest was watching him, his eyebrows raised questioningly. Walsh looked at them both. He knew they were sharing some secret between them but had no idea what it was.

'Like what?' he demanded.

'Like I couldn't fail to score from them,' Chris said, a little clumsily.

'Too right,' Walsh agreed. 'That last one, the goalkeeper dived so early, the game hadn't even started. Hey, Mac – I want a word with you.'

Walsh went off to give Mac some advice about always standing up until the last moment when a forward was coming in one on one. Chris heard him say 'make yourself a big target', which was pretty funny if you were watching and could see that Mac was about half his size.

Mac had a 'Now what have I done?' expression on his face. He was clearly confused by this advice, particularly seeing as Eastbury's goal had come from a deflected free kick.

'It always makes me laugh watching those two talk,' commented Priest. 'Mac always gets confused by about the second sentence, and Iain can't understand Mac's accent.'

Chris agreed. Most often, he had to act like an interpreter, explaining the coach's plans to Mac, or repeating what the tiny keeper had just said, without the heavy Scottish burr.

'Good game today,' said Priest, smiling. 'If we're going to be this hard to stop at home, I think it'll rub off on our away form too. Javinder's a good find, Chris. Is there anyone else at Spirebrook I should be looking at?'

The only other quality player at school was Phil Lucas, and he wasn't going to get a look-in while Riverside had Rory. The one thing the area around Spirebrook had in abundance was strikers, it seemed.

'I can't help you, I'm afraid,' he confessed.

'Well, keep your eye out during your school games. We need someone with a bit of bite in midfield, and maybe another defender. What do you think?'

'Someone a bit taller wouldn't go amiss, just to help out at set pieces and stuff.'

'That's what I thought. Let me know if you see anyone.'

Priest wandered off to speak to some of the others. Chris found Javinder wearily unlacing his boots on the clubhouse steps.

'A bit faster here, isn't it?' asked Chris.

'I'm knackered!' gasped Javinder. 'When I brought the ball out of defence that last time, I thought I was going to die before I got to the halfway line.'

Chris pulled him up. 'You did well,' he told his new playing partner. 'You were involved in almost every move, and that was a great pass through the defence for the fourth goal.'

'Yeah? I thought I'd over-hit it. You and Nicky always seemed to have this understanding . . . the ball –'

'Jazz,' said Chris, cutting him off firmly. 'Nicky isn't here.'

And with that, he left Jazz on the steps and went inside to change.

Eighteen

The following Thursday, Spirebrook opened their season with the match against their old rivals, Blackmoor. Flea drove them across the city in the mini-bus, giving them some last-minute advice. Chris watched the world go by through the window.

As games went, it wasn't up to much. In fact, it had the feel of a 0–0 draw from the moment Blackmoor took the kick-off. Their pitch was even worse than Spirebrook's; a heavy slab of clay with patches of long grass in some places and hard black earth in others. It was like running through quicksand one second and then on concrete the next. Worse still, the ball bounced wildly all over the place, making it impossible to control. Chris had one sight of goal all match, when a defender headed the ball out and Chris raced in to hit the volley. The ball hopped up off a twist of yellow grass and Chris hit it off his shin. It flew about 30 metres wide, causing more danger to the corner flag than the goal.

A ragged chorus of jeers echoed from a group of black-jacketed spectators over on the touchline. Bearing in mind that no Blackmoor player got even that close to scoring, it was a bit rich.

As it turned out, there was only one reason to remember the game, and that came after the final whistle. While the others were finishing getting changed, Chris asked for permission to run to a newsagent opposite the school gates so he could get the *Oldcester Post* to check out United's team for the first-round Coca-Cola tie that night. Flea told him to hurry.

As he jogged through the gates, Chris heard a shout from behind him. He ignored it and went into the shop. He was reading the back page of the paper as he came out. It took him a few moments to realise that there was a ring of Blackmoor students blocking the exit.

He looked up. The first one he recognised was the ginger-headed moron from the bus stop almost seven months before. The others were all there – the blond guy who played in the football team, the hard-faced fifth-former who had pinned Nicky against the shelter and the giggling idiot with the earring.

'Where's your pal?' sneered Ginger.

'Who are we talking about?' asked Chris defensively, even though he knew full well.

'The greasy prat who normally plays with you lot. Thinks he's tasty, only the one thing he's good at is shooting his mouth off.'

'Oh, him,' said Chris, without adding anything else. Well, what a surprise. Nicky wasn't even here and he was still getting Chris into trouble. What would it take to get Fiorentini out of his life for good?

Ginger had started to suspect that Chris was being dense on purpose. He stepped closer.

'You were lucky that big mouth of yours didn't get you into trouble last year.' he snarled. 'But there's nowhere to run to this time.'

'Really?' said Chris, his expression suddenly very worried. 'Oh, dear!'

Ginger started to reach out to grab him, but Chris had already stepped quickly back through the shop doorway.

As they started to follow, Chris wagged his finger in Ginger's face and then pointed at a sign in the window. 'No more than two students in the shop at once!' he said loudly, and he heard the shopkeeper calling to them as well, telling them he didn't want trouble on his premises and that he'd speak to their head teacher if they didn't clear off.

Ginger's face had gone bright red and he looked as if he was all for going through the door after Chris anyway, but the others held him back. Looking across the road, Chris could see that the Spirebrook mini-bus was filling up, and Flea was waiting for him to come back. He could just sit tight and the cavalry would arrive any minute.

123

'Forget it!' he heard the blond guy tell the others. 'This isn't who we were looking for anyway. It's the other one we want.'

They were starting to step back — the trouble was over. But inside Chris, something had just snapped.

He took a long stride through the doorway and into the middle of the small cluster of black-coated students. Before they even knew he was there, he had tapped the blond kid on the shoulder.

'Excuse me,' he said, 'but did I hear you say you were looking for my mate?'

'What of it?' said Blondy, who clearly hadn't expected to see Chris again.

'He said you might be here looking for him,' Chris said, 'but he couldn't make it.'

'Scared, was he?' asked Ginger.

'No, but he said he wanted to make it a fair fight. So he was going to send his kid sister instead. That would be about right for four of you —'

The guys from Blackmoor might have been slow, but they weren't *that* slow. Blondy leapt at Chris from the side and Ginger threw a fist which Chris half-blocked, though it still smacked him in the eye. He lashed out with his own fists, and shook himself loose of their grip, rolling across the pavement.

As he got up, he could hear Flea yelling from the school driveway, getting closer. Ginger had a bloodied nose, and was alternately whingeing about it and threatening to smash Chris to a pulp. The others were ready for more, but the rapid approach of Flea and the shopkeeper meant hostilities were going to have to be postponed.

'I'll have you!' snarled Blondy, pointing.

'Saturday, Loam Park, two o'clock,' snapped Chris quickly. 'One on one, or do you need your girlfriends to hold your hands?'

'You and me will be fine,' Blondy said, grinning. 'You better be there.'

'I'll be there,' snapped Chris, before Flea arrived on the scene to calm things down and lead him away.

'That'll bruise,' the PE teacher observed briskly as they walked back towards the mini-bus. 'Fancy getting into a fight,

Chris! What will your father say?'

He started with, 'What was it all about?'

Chris shrugged, and tried to make as light of the fight as he could. It really wasn't something he wanted to have to explain.

'Nothing. They're just kids from Blackmoor, trying to look hard. You know these posh schools where they have entrance exams to get in? Well, at Blackmoor, they ask you if you can add two and two together without using your fingers, and if you fail, they let you in.'

'Maybe we should send you there,' said his father, clearly in no mood for joking. He turned Chris's head to one side so that he could inspect the black eye more closely.

'That's going to look wonderful in the morning.'

'It feels pretty gruesome right now.'

'Serves you right.'

Chris's father dabbed something on the bruised skin, for no better reason than it stung like crazy, as far as Chris could tell.

'Ow!'

'Keep still and it won't hurt.'

Parents, thought Chris. They do talk some rubbish. He kept still – and quiet – anyway.

'Couldn't you have avoided the trouble?'

'Not really. They were lined up outside the shop.'

'What did they want?'

'Nothing.'

Chris's father dabbed at the wound again. This must be how the Gestapo got people to talk, Chris decided. His father had that wounded 'I thought we could talk about these kinds of things' expression on his face that he only wore when he was really annoyed.

'Is this the same lot you had that trouble with last year?'

'What lot?'

'The lot that roughed you and Nicky around before school one morning, and threw your bag up on the garages.'

'How did you know about that?' cried Chris, utterly amazed.

'Baynham told me. I cut his breakfast allowance until he cracked.'

'Torture is illegal,' muttered Chris.

'Tell that to the United Nations,' said his father, dabbing some more of the sickly antiseptic on to his face.

When he had finished playing paramedic, Mr Stephens put the first aid kit away, and they both went into the kitchen to start preparing dinner. Pizza, sweetcorn and potatoes. It was unusual for them to eat something like that on a night when Chris's father wasn't working late. Perhaps he was going out again in the evening.

'I'm right, aren't I?' he asked, shifting Chris's attention back to the incident after the match. 'They're the same guys, right? The ones that ripped your sleeve off?'

'Yes,' said Chris, waiting for the oven to preheat.

'Last time they were after Nicky, right, and you got dragged in?'

'Uh-huh,' Chris replied, trying to look busy by reading the instructions on the pizza box. He didn't like where this was heading.

'So what was it about this time?'

Chris looked up. There was no point trying to avoid this. 'I can't make you understand, Dad, so don't make me try. They were looking for Nicky and they found me. That's all.'

Chris's father clearly wanted to hear more, but Chris was determined not to tell him. How could he? He didn't understand it himself. One minute, the gang were about to leave him alone because it was Nicky they were after, not him. Next minute, he'd been thinking that he couldn't even get beaten up on his own; that it was still all Nicky, Nicky, Nicky. And so, to prove that he was just as worth smacking around as anybody, Chris had thrown himself at them.

How could he admit that to anyone, himself included? He got beaten up because they didn't want to beat him up, and that made him mad.

Mad nothing. He was stupid.

Thankfully, Chris's father reacted to his outburst by dropping the subject, at least for now. They ate, watched *Home Improvements* (a repeat, but it was a good one), then washed up.

'Go and get changed, will you, Chris? We're stepping out for a while. I put some clean clothes on your bed.'

'Where are we going?'

'I can't explain, son, so don't make me try. Just go and get out of those school clothes, OK?'

Twenty minutes later, the car started at the third attempt (which was better than average), and they were heading down towards the main road, and turning right, heading for the bustling centre of Spirebrook.

The dry cleaners, the building society and the undertakers were all closed, of course, but it had never been likely that this was a shopping expedition. Chris's father steered the car left at the new traffic lights, away from the new Safeway and up Church Hill towards –

Oh no.

Moments later, they pulled to a stop outside a smart detached house with two big trees in the long front yard, a satellite dish on the chimney breast and a Mercedes parked outside the garage.

Chris didn't have time to protest. Uncle Fabian had opened the door and was advancing towards them with a can of Diet Coke in his hand and a warm smile across his face.

'Great, you made it just in time!' he said, beaming. 'Come on in, the match is about to start.'

⚽

A friend of Fabian's sister's husband installed Sky TV for a living. He'd fixed the Fiorentini household up with the complete works for next to nothing. They had wide-screen stereo TV, and Nicky's mother always made enough food to feed three times as many visitors as there were.

Chris had been there to watch games plenty of times before. But that was then, before everything that had happened last spring. This was now.

'Good surprise, eh?' said Chris's father. 'I bumped into Fabian when I went into the bank in the city centre at lunchtime. He invited us to watch the game live.'

'Great!' said Chris, as enthusiastically as he could manage.

'Of course, no Des, Jimmy or Alan this way, but you can't have everything, eh?'

Uncle Fabian was laughing as if this was a great joke and Chris had been suckered all the way in. The rest of the Fiorentini clan joined in, and Chris had to just grin and bear it.

The living room was large, with an arch knocked through to what had once been a separate dining room. Even so, the Fiorentini family managed to fill it. Nicky's mother and father, the baby (now a loud four-year-old), both the sisters, Uncle Fabian, one of the cousins who lived in Enfield (not the one with the American car, this was the one who fitted double glazing), Grandma Fiorentini, a cousin Chris had never seen before and her boyfriend from Coventry, a neighbour named Charlie and two insane Alsatians squeezed on to chairs, the settee, some folding seats and the floor, ready to watch Manchester United against Port Vale.

When Des and Jimmy and Alan appeared, Chris's father was very confused.

'It's BBC1,' Chris informed him. 'It's not on satellite. We could have watched this at home.'

'Ah, yes, but we have wide-screen and stereo!' boomed Uncle Fabian, who missed any possible insult in Chris's remark. 'And we have sandwiches!'

Mrs Fiorentini fetched in a huge platter of chicken in French bread, and everyone cheered.

Well, there was no way they could leave, so Chris decided he might as well enjoy it. The sandwiches were wonderful, and the TV picture was pin-sharp. It might only have been a Coca-Cola first round tie, but it was the biggest TV game Chris had ever seen. The players were almost as large as the people in the room watching.

Uncle Fabian lowered himself into the chair beside Chris, his diet cola in one hand and a vast sandwich in the other.

'Nicky says everyone is really excited about this game. Who knows, perhaps we'll see him in the crowd, eh?'

They didn't, and Chris tried hard not to try. The game was a good one, and Chris was kept well supplied with cola and food to tide him over any stoppage periods. Having made a slight blunder in the away leg, Manchester United were in great form and blew Port Vale away after a nervous start. John

128

Motson was gushing, Trevor Brooking was speechless. It was just as well, because the Fiorentinis kept up eight different commentaries of their own, scarcely stopping to draw breath.

'Pretty good, eh?' said Uncle Fabian, nudging Chris in the ribs at half-time. 'What will they be like when Nicky joins them?'

'Older?' asked Chris, mischievously. Uncle Fabian thought this was extremely amusing.

'Help me carry some of these plates through into the kitchen, Chris,' he said, still chuckling. Somehow, the mounds of food had been disappearing, and Chris found himself heaped with empty crockery, following Uncle Fabian (carrying two tea cups) out into the kitchen.

The women, who were huddled by the back door, went out into the conservatory as they went into the kitchen. A few furtive glances had been exchanged. Chris, suddenly reminded of scenes from The Godfather, began to wonder if this was some kind of trap (he'd be gunned down by the sink while Cousin Luke strangled his father in the living room — perhaps he'd kick through the TV screen in his death throes). Maybe all this friendly behaviour had been designed to put them off their guard; perhaps they all knew that he and Nicky had become mortal enemies. Uncle Fabian shut the hall door, and the trap was closed.

It was a trap, but not the one Chris expected. Uncle Fabian, it turned out, wanted a favour.

'I'm glad we have this chance to talk, Chris. It's a pity we don't see so much of you now, since Nicky moved away.' Chris was warily watching Uncle Fabian handle a bread knife. 'Now you're here, I need to ask you a favour.'

'Of course,' said Chris quickly, still caught up in his imagination.

'Nicky hasn't been home these last few weekends, and he hasn't been telephoning so often. My sister, Clara, she's getting a bit worried. She says he isn't as happy as she expected.'

Chris suddenly realised he needed to visit the loo. It must have been all the cola. 'That's a shame,' he commented.

'He hasn't said anything to you?' Uncle Fabian continued, fishing for information.

'I don't hear anything from him at all,' replied Chris.

Uncle Fabian's face lit up as if he had just seen another clue in a great mystery. 'You see!' he cried. 'He doesn't even call his best friend any more. Don't you think that's strange?'

'Not rea–' Chris started to say, but he bit his lip.

This business with Nicky was really strange. Not just the business with him not coming home or phoning, which was weird enough, but the fact that Nicky hadn't told anyone about the way he and Chris had parted company. Listening to Uncle Fabian, it was just as if Chris and Nicky were still the same old duo, even though separated by a few hundred miles.

Nicky hadn't told anyone and Chris hadn't told anyone. It was like a shared secret, the sort of thing –

Uncle Fabian interrupted before Chris got much further along that road. Chris could see that he was genuinely worried about Nicky.

'What do you think has happened, Chris?'

'I honestly don't know, Unc– Mr Fiorentini.'

Uncle Fabian sighed, and wiped his hands on a tea towel.

'It doesn't make sense, you know? It doesn't feel right. His mother and father, they'd like to go up there and find out; I'd like to go up there myself, but Nicky wouldn't tell me. He wouldn't tell anybody. You boys, you keep your secrets locked away inside. You don't tell anyone anything – except each other.'

This was the phrase that suddenly made it all very clear what was coming. Chris's mind went on-line, switching on extra RAM, SVGA graphics and Soundblaster sound, desperately looking for a way out of the trap he had blundered into. It was just a pity that his speech software was bugged.

'Unc– Fab– Mr Fiorentini, I – I –'

'Hear me out, Chris. On Saturday, Manchester United play Aston Villa. Nicky has got tickets. I said I'd go up there and go with him to the game. He thinks I'll bring Luke with me, you see? So, instead, I take you. It'll be a big surprise for Nicky, you see? Then, after the game, we go and have a hamburger, and you two can talk, and you can find out what is really going on.'

'Yes — yes, we *could*, only I — I — errr —.' Inspiration flickered briefly, and he snatched at it. 'I have an appointment, Saturday.'

That's right, 2pm, Loam Park, he was due to get beaten up because Nicky wasn't there to get beaten up, and because he, Chris, was a second-best target for their hatred.

'Really?' said Uncle Fabian. 'Can't you move it?'

'No. Too important. And besides, I wouldn't be allowed to go anywhere else because I'm grounded. For fighting. See?' He pointed at his black eye. Uncle Fabian stared at it as if he had only just noticed it was there. His moustache lifted up and exposed a broad grin.

'You boys, always fighting! How does the other guy look, eh?' Uncle Fabian directed a soft punch at the side of Chris's head, which he was almost too muddle-headed to duck under. 'Don't you worry, Chris. I have a lot of experience in getting fathers to change their minds about these things. If it wasn't for me, Nicky would have been locked in the attic half his life! I'll speak to your father, get him to agree, and in return, you'll come with me Saturday, all right? Help me solve this problem?' Chris had run out of excuses. Uncle Fabian clearly took the silence to mean that Chris agreed. He slapped him on the back, and loaded him up with more plates to carry back into the living room. 'I knew I could depend on you, Chris. You and Nicky are a team, right? And you always have to work for the team.'

Sure, thought Chris, as he staggered back to his place under the weight of the food. The second half was just kicking off. Uncle Fabian gestured with his eyes towards the screen, and smiled as if to say, 'Saturday, we'll be there.' Chris tried to smile back.

Perhaps, if he was dead lucky, he'd be struck by lightning first.

Nineteen

'You're not grounded,' his father said two evenings later.

'I know,' said Chris.

'You were playing football after school last night, weren't you? You can't be grounded.'

'I know,' said Chris again, with more determination. He tried to look as if he was concentrating on the TV – he was using Ceefax to search for the draw for the second round of the Coca-Cola Cup. The pages were scrolling incredibly slowly. Finally, it reached the page he was looking for. Oldcester's game was the third on the list. 'Manchester United!' he gasped.

'I know. Fabian Fiorentini called me at work. Said he wanted to take you to Manchester United tomorrow, and was it all right with me if you went. He seemed to think you were grounded –'

'No!' said Chris. 'Oldcester have got Manchester United in the next round. I don't believe it!'

His father peered at the TV. 'Now there's a coincidence,' he said. 'I'd better think about getting tickets – it'll be a sell-out down here. Anyway, you're going, right?'

'I thought you said you had to get tickets?'

'Not to the football! I meant you're going to Manchester with Uncle Fabian. To see Nicky and –' Chris's father stopped as he realised he was talking about football after all.

'OK, OK.'

'I'm glad we've cleared that up,' Mr Stephens muttered, leaving the room after a world record-breaking confusing conversation. Chris was feeling more than a little confused himself. What on earth was he doing agreeing to go up to see Nicky? What possible good could it do?

If this lightning was coming, it needed to come really soon.

The weather stayed brilliantly clear and fine, and Uncle Fabian steered the car on to the motorway and started heading north. The car was luxurious, with leather seats and gleaming dials, and Chris could have really enjoyed the ride if he hadn't known the destination.

'Put some music on, if you like,' Uncle Fabian said, gesturing towards the glove compartment.

Chris opened it, half-expecting to find CDs of Pavarotti singing operas in Italian. Instead, it was stuffed with Iron Maiden, Def Leppard and Deep Purple.

'Are these all Luke's?' asked Chris.

'No, mine!' replied Uncle Fabian, in a hurt voice that suggested he was offended by any suggestion that he and his son shared the same taste in music.

Chris found the new Oasis CD at the top of the pile. It was the nearest thing he could find to something he had heard.

The sound system in the car was beefed up wickedly, and Chris could feel his fillings vibrating as the first track began.

Uncle Fabian sang along. He sounded a bit like Pavarotti, even singing heavy rock. Chris laughed, and when the current single started, he joined in as well.

The Mercedes roadshow thundered up the road.

'What do you mean, he's not here?' thundered Uncle Fabian.

The woman, his sister Clara (and the only Fiorentini Chris had ever seen who didn't have night-black hair), was whimpering in her chair, clutching a cup of black coffee in one hand and a handkerchief in the other.

'It's not my fault,' she wailed. 'I told him you were coming!'

'What did he say?'

'He said he couldn't go to the game because he had to go and see someone. A friend, he said. He left you the tickets.'

Uncle Fabian was holding them in his hand and glowering angrily, sharing his wrathful glare equally between the tickets and his skinny, weeping sister.

'But I've brought Chris all this way!'

'He didn't know that!'

'Of course not,' thundered Uncle Fabian. 'It was a surprise!!!'

Clara wailed again, and Uncle Fabian rolled his eyes up to the ceiling. Chris expected him to say 'Mama Mia' or something like that, but instead he cried out 'I just don't believe it!', which sounded so much like that old guy on the TV it made Chris giggle. He stifled it just in time. Uncle Fabian was glaring at him. 'Perhaps he has gone to the game already, or someone at the ground knows where he has gone. I will go and find out.'

'OK.' Chris started to rise.

'No, stay here in case he comes back. Ring me on the car phone.'

Chris opened his mouth to protest, but couldn't think of any suggestion that made better sense. Besides, this didn't feel like a good time to argue. Uncle Fabian gripped his car keys tightly in his fist and stormed out.

Clara sobbed even louder. She slowly calmed down as the Mercedes pulled away, dabbing at her cheeks with a sopping wet tissue that didn't so much mop anything up as spread it around evenly. Chris suddenly remembered just how mad the traffic was likely to be around Old Trafford, but it was too late to warn Uncle Fabian now, and he didn't want to ask Clara for the number in case it started her off again.

Twenty minutes later, a phone call from Uncle Fabian did start her off again. He was stuck in traffic and it was all her fault.

Clara was weeping up a storm by the time she put the phone down. Chris's ears still hurt from 120 miles of heavy metal. He couldn't take this. She started moaning about how Nicky had been giving her trouble from the first day that he arrived, and that it was her fault and that she'd tried to make sure he went to school every day, but she knew that he hadn't and she was sure he was getting into trouble with some other boys and —

'Mrs Fiorentini . . .' Chris interrupted.

'O'Malley,' she replied, snappily, yet still managing to add a few more tears to her hankie.

'I'm sorry?'

134

'O'Malley. I'm married.'

'Oh, right.' Chris drew a deep breath and started again. 'Mrs O'Malley, is there some other friend of Nicky's, someone who lives round here, someone who might know where he is?'

'Sure,' she said. 'He has plenty of friends at school. They hang around the shopping precinct most of the time.'

'Well, I'll go and have a look there,' said Chris, rising to his feet and edging towards the door. 'Just show me which way it is, and I'll be there and back in ten minutes.'

'It's just before the main road . . . about a mile. You can't miss it.'

Mrs O'Malley lived on one of those new out-of-town village estates which had a small pedestrian-only shopping centre in the centre, and a winding road around the outside that everyone drove along on their way out of the village towards the nearest superstores and shopping centres in Bolton or Manchester. The precinct was inhabited by eight scruffy shops, including a chippy, an off-licence and an estate agent (just like Spirebrook, only without the undertaker), and outside were clustered about twenty kids of ages ranging from five to fifteen.

Chris had jogged across the estate, following the signs, getting lost twice, but finding his way into the precinct at last. The kids all looked at him, realising that he didn't belong. However, the only one that looked at all aggressive was about eight and was blowing bubble gum.

'Any of you lot know Nicky Fiorentini?'

'Nicky who?' asked the gum blower.

Chris pondered this for a moment. Perhaps expecting Nicky to be famous was a bit much.

'About my age . . . black hair . . . plays football.'

'He's useless at football,' said the eight-year-old, who had a shaved head and an earring, and who was clearly dead hard.

'You know who I mean?' asked Chris.

'No.'

'Oh, shut up, Davey,' said one of the older girls, slapping the boy round the back of the head so hard his gum popped out. He looked up at her with a hurt expression on his face. 'You mean Nicky who lives with Mrs O'Malley?' the girl said, turning her attention back to Chris.

'That's right.'

The girl looked at her friends, who all looked at each other. Chris felt certain they knew something. 'He's in Bolton, with the Telford brothers.'

'Bolton?'

'Yeah. There's a big shopping centre –'

'Nicky's gone shopping?' laughed Chris, who couldn't imagine anything less likely.

'Not exactly,' said the girl, who was looking increasingly sheepish. Chris doubted that she was going to say any more, and yet he had no other way of finding out what she was hiding. There was a long silence in which Chris prayed that someone – anyone – would say something. Fortunately, Davey was still in a sulky mood after being cuffed round the ear, and he chimed in with the truth.

'Shop-lifting, more like!'

'What?!'

'You heard! Your mate's gone to Bolton to nick stuff!'

Chris stood there, mouth agape, trying to take this in. Could Davey be lying or have got it wrong? He doubted it. The little toe-rag had a malicious grin on his impish face that made it very likely that he was telling the truth.

'How do I get to Bolton from here?' asked Chris, quickly.

'There's a bus from Victoria Street,' said the girl.

'Show me,' said Chris, and, as they had nothing else to do, the whole pack of them – even Davey – led him to the bus stop and waited to make sure he got on the right one. None of them, though, could be persuaded to tell him anything more. They all seemed frightened of the Telford brothers, especially Davey, who was looking sorry that he'd said anything.

The girl promised to go and tell Clara where Chris had gone. Between the twenty of them, they even managed to come up with £3.40 to lend him. He promised to pay them back.

'Be careful!' said the oldest girl, as the doors closed behind him.

Don't worry, thought Chris, glancing at his watch. I'm supposed to be getting a working over at two o'clock anyway.

136

Twenty

The centre of Bolton was filled with shoppers, and Chris knew from the moment he stepped off the bus that this was going to be like trying to find a needle in a haystack. He went back and forth along every street, wandering round the larger stores, checking out the hamburger bars and the arcades, searching for a glimpse of Nicky's black-haired head. It was hopeless. Chris realised that his plan needed an enormous amount of luck if it was going to succeed, and today didn't feel like it was his lucky day.

After three hours, Chris realised luck wasn't on his side. It was 4.45pm. He should have been leaving Old Trafford about now. No, what he should have been doing was settling in the armchair at home, having just laid out all four of the Blackmoor morons, ready to watch *Final Score* on the TV.

Final Score.

It was an inspired guess, and it paid off. There was a Granada TV rental shop about 50 metres up the road, and as Chris raced for it, his heart leapt with joy. Outside, gazing in at the window, was a forlorn figure in smart jeans, a United jersey under a black denim jacket and a baseball cap.

'Nicky!'

Nicky looked up as he heard the call, then his face widened in amazement as he realised who was calling. He moved quickly, startled, as if he was going to try and make a break for it, but Chris closed the gap on him too fast. He grabbed Nicky by the arm and pulled him back.

'Hey – hang on! Where are you going in such a hurry?'

Nicky's face was dark with anger, and something else. He tried to shake Chris loose. 'Get lost, Chris. You don't belong here.'

'Right. And you do.' Chris hung on determinedly.

'I mean it, Chris. There'll only be trouble if you stay.'

'From the Telford brothers?' asked Chris.

Nicky stopped struggling. The ferocity went out of his eyes and he sighed, clearly knowing that Chris wasn't going to let him go. He still seemed very jumpy to Chris, but perhaps that wasn't surprising.

'How much do you know?' he asked.

Chris relaxed his grip and tried to pull his thoughts together. It seemed best to tell Nicky the whole story.

'Your Uncle Fabian drove me up here this morning. It wasn't my idea – but your family is worried because you don't come home weekends or phone very often. I said I didn't hear from you either, but all that did was convince them even more that something was wrong.

'So, Uncle Fabian thought all three of us could go to the football, and then I was supposed to ask you what the problem was after the game while we had a jolly meal in Burger King.'

Nicky chuckled, though he still looked a little edgy, glancing around them. Chris looked through the shop window and saw the teleprinter was still running.

'Anyway,' Chris continued, 'we arrived at your aunt's house and you weren't there. Uncle Fabian is looking for you in Manchester, and I met up with some kids on the estate who said you'd come here.'

'Great. I bet Amy Baxter was one of them. She just can't keep her mouth shut.'

'If Amy has a geek of a brother called Davey, she's one of them, yes.'

Nicky nodded. They both looked towards the TVs in the shop.

'That explains it, then,' sighed Nicky.

'Partly . . .' said Chris. 'Nicky, why have you never told anyone in your family about the fight we had? They still think we're the best of friends!'

Nicky turned quickly and his temper flared again. He opened his mouth to speak but the words didn't come. After a few seconds, the fire burned out and he looked back through the window.

'I just didn't, OK? Leave it at that.'

Chris decided that was just what he wanted to do. A few Third Division results passed through the teleprinter, followed by a win for Chelsea at home. They watched in silence.

Finally, Chris became impatient.

'So, seeing as I've been dragged halfway up the country, not to mention hauling myself to a town I've never been to just so I could find you, think you might tell me what's going on?'

'Why?'

It was Chris's turn to feel his temper rise. 'Just tell me, Nicky! I know why you're here. Shop-lifting!' He realised too late that he had said that last word rather loudly. A few passers-by turned their heads, but fortunately no-one stopped. 'Shop-lifting,' he said again, much more softly. 'Are you crazy? And from what I hear, you've been wagging school and stuff like that.'

'You wouldn't understand.'

'There's a lot of things I don't understand about you any more, Nicky. I don't understand why you turned on me, why you tried to make sure we lost the final, why you planted those pills in my bag . . . But there's one thing I do understand. If Manchester United find out you're into nicking stuff, they'll drop you. You'll be finished. Is that what you want, Nicky?'

Nicky looked up, and Chris could see that there were angry tears in his eyes. At once, he started to realise what must have happened.

'I failed the trials. They said I wasn't a good enough team player, that I only looked after my own interests. Told me I'd be a good school player, but never anything more than that . . .'

'But you've been telling your family —'

'I had to tell them what they wanted to hear. If anyone came up, I'd get them tickets for the game. Aunt Clara didn't know what was going on — I went out three nights a week, just like when I was training. No-one had to know anything.'

'Why couldn't you just come home?'

Their eyes met. The answer didn't need to be said.

Another long silence, and the teleprinter rolled on. Chris nearly spoke when he saw that Oldcester had won away, but he kept quiet.

'I couldn't tell them that I failed,' Nicky said quietly.

Chris understood, up to a point. He wondered just how long Nicky could have kept up this double life, but there was no point getting into that now.

'OK,' he said, cutting through the confusion as best he could. 'I can handle all that, but I still don't understand why you're into nicking stuff!'

Nicky glanced around again. Chris knew he was hiding from someone, or looking for them.

'When I wasn't training, I needed something to do. So I started hanging round with the other kids on the estate. They're all right, I guess, and we didn't get into any trouble or anything. But then I lost some tickets Uncle Fabian had paid for, and I had to get some more. I borrowed the money.'

Chris still couldn't quite see. 'And?'

'And I borrowed it from the Telford brothers. They live on the estate too, and all the kids are scared of them. They're bad news, Chris.'

Final Score had started, and the Premiership scores went up. Manchester United had won 3–0.

'Wish we'd gone,' said Nicky.

'Me too,' agreed Chris. 'Anything would be better than schlepping around here. Honestly, Nicky, you are a prat. What on earth is so special about these Telford brothers?'

'Why don't you ask one of them, mate?' a voice replied. Nicky jumped as if he had been stung by a wasp, and Chris turned round – and up – to look into an ugly, sneering pale face with piggy eyes.

'Hello, Nicky,' said the youth. 'We've been looking all over for you. Aren't you going to introduce us to your mate?'

Nicky chose not to say anything. For the moment, fighting his natural inclination to come up with some witty and potentially hazardous remark, Chris kept his mouth shut too.

'My name's Barry Telford,' said Pig-face, finishing the introduction with a sniff. 'Who are you?'

'A mate of Nicky's.'

'Nicky doesn't have any mates, do you, Nicky?' Nicky still remained silent. 'Of course, he doesn't need proper mates because he's got us, and we look after him.'

The youth was at least ten inches taller than Chris and he must have weighed twice as much. Chris guessed he was about seventeen, with the mental age of someone of about five.

'He's got mates back home, in Oldcester.'

'Oldcester? That scabby little town? Sounds like something you'd make up does Oldcester. Not a real town, not like Bolton.'

Barry was wearing a Wanderers shirt. Chris felt an idea ping into his brain.

'Maybe, but that's where Nicky comes from and so do I. And we're going back there tonight.'

It sounded so easy when you just said it like that. Chris wondered how to make it come true. From where he was standing in the doorway, he couldn't even see daylight around Barry Telford.

'Now, you see, that's where you're wrong. Nicky can't be leaving just yet, because he still owes us some money. That means he's got to nick a whole lot more stuff for us.' Pig-face lifted a heavy sports bag he was carrying in one hand. Chris heard stuff shifting around inside it. 'Besides, now he's seen how much fun it is living up here, he's never going to want to go back to some little hole like Oldcester.'

'It may be a hole,' said Chris, 'but we were still good enough to beat Bolton today.'

Telford's face fell and twisted in a pathetic grimace. 'We've not lost, have we?' he wailed, stepping forward to look into the window.

'Nicky, RUN!!!' yelled Chris, and he dived into the gap behind Telford's back, grabbing Nicky's arm and pulling him through after him. They leapt out on to the pavement and sprinted up the street.

Chris knew Pig-face would be able to out-run them, but not with that heavy bag in his fist. He was gambling that they could put enough space between them and him and that he wouldn't dare drop the bag to go after them.

Chris and Nicky had always been quick, but they were running quicker now than ever before. Dodging through the crowds, they blasted along the main shopping streets, trying to lose themselves in a sea of faces. Behind them, they heard Barry Telford yelling and cursing at their backs, trying to push his way through the reluctant throng.

They turned into a smaller street, climbing a steep hill. They were about halfway up when they heard him shout again. Looking back, they saw him at the bottom of the slope, about 100 metres away.

'This way!' said Nicky. The chase continued.

They dashed up and down, left and right, trying to put as many corners as they could between them and their pursuer so that he couldn't be sure which way they'd gone. They raced through the bus station, along some old, terraced streets, and through the gates of a cemetery.

By now they were gasping for breath. They circled down behind the weather-beaten, soot-stained church, and fell into a heap behind a large gravestone, shaded by the low branches of a small tree.

'Do you think we lost him?' gasped Nicky.

'I think we lost us,' moaned Chris, trying to peer around the edge of the gravestone towards the gate. 'Tell me you know your way round Bolton.'

'I'm afraid not.'

'Then why were you telling me which way to go?'

Nicky shrugged. 'It just seemed like a good idea at the time.'

He burrowed in his jacket pocket and pulled out a couple of chocolate bars, handing one to Chris.

'Did you pinch these?' Chris asked dubiously.

'It still tastes the same!' snapped Nicky.

'No, it doesn't.'

'Fine. Go without, then. Although, as it happens, I paid for them.'

Chris took the bar Nicky was still holding out for him. He was starving. Clara must have been the only Fiorentini in the universe who didn't force-feed people the moment they came through her door.

'How long shall we leave it?'

'A while yet,' said Nicky. 'The Telfords may be stupid, but they're very patient.'

'OK. We wait then. As soon as we're sure we're safe, we

call Uncle Fabian from a call box and get him to come and get us.'

'Good plan,' agreed Nicky. They settled down to wait.

Chocolate bars only last so long, and silence is oppressive (especially in a graveyard). Chris knew he was going to have to ask Nicky about what had happened the year before. He just couldn't see where to start.

'I knew you wouldn't get into trouble,' Nicky whispered.

Chris shifted so that he could see him, and still keep an eye on the cemetery gates. 'How's that?'

'The pills. They were bound to check what they were.'

'That took a couple of days, Nicky!'

'But they found out in the end right? They were asthma pills. My sister-in-law's.'

'And the packet?'

'Luke brought it home a year or so ago. Someone had been peddling the real stuff to some athletes down his way. He brought the box to show Uncle Fabian, so he could ask him what to do.'

'Did they do anything?'

'No. Uncle Fabian said someone might think Luke was involved. He showed me the box to warn me against ever getting into stuff like that. I kept it in a drawer in my bedroom.'

Chris sniffed, and lowered his head to the grass. He knew he would never forget that moment when the box had tumbled from the split-open bag and everyone had looked at him.

'OK. That explains the pills. Now what about the game, Nicky?'

'What about it?'

'You were playing to lose, Nicky! Not bad enough that it was obvious, not bad enough to make yourself *look* bad, but bad enough to make sure we couldn't score. Bad enough to make sure we lost.'

'Hang on, we scored three. And I got two of them!'

'One was a penalty, Nicky. Pretty hard to fake.'

'At least I scored mine, and the one in the shoot-out. Are you saying I arranged things so that you'd miss the one you took?'

'If you hadn't been pratting about, we wouldn't have

needed a penalty shoot-out.'

'Oh, right. And what about the first half hour, when you were crawling around like a one-legged dog and I was running all over them. I got us back in the game!'

'We were two—nil down by then, Nicky!'

'I still did more to give us a chance of a result than you, even though I had two of them marking me!'

'What?!'

'I scored the goal that tied the game too!'

'You even admitted you stole that from me! Jeez, Nicky, you did everything you could to make it look like it was me muffing all the chances. I worked my guts out trying to make a few openings, but every pass you hit me all day was off-target.'

'Don't talk stupid! You were like a zombie all match. Any other day and you would have been on every pass.'

'Who's fault is that! I was still half dead from when you tried to dump me in the naffing river!'

Nicky didn't reply. Chris realised they had been getting louder and more heated, the longer the argument went on. Barry Telford would have heard every word five miles away.

'This is bright,' said Nicky. 'We hide in a graveyard and then yell our heads off.' He tapped the gravestone with the back of his hand. 'Even some of these guys are complaining about the noise.'

Chris gave a short laugh, then peered around the gravestone. There was still no sign of anybody, except a chubby bloke in church vestments, walking over on the far side of the graveyard. The man stopped to pull a few weeds from the ground.

'Think he heard us?'

Nicky shrugged. 'Who knows? Who cares? It's the Telfords we have to worry about.'

'No sign of anybody,' muttered Chris, thankfully. 'Maybe we really did lose him.'

'Maybe,' said Nicky. Neither of them made any move to leave.

Chris glanced at his watch. It was coming up to six o'clock. Just how long were they prepared to hide out in here? It wouldn't be dark for another hour; hour and a half, maybe.

144

He turned to face Nicky again.

'All right. Maybe I was wrong about you wanting to lose the game —'

'Now, I didn't say that,' Nicky said, with a slight grin on his face. Chris was about ready to hit him. Nicky threw his hands over his head for protection. 'I admit I wanted to make you look bad,' Nicky continued, peering out from under his arms. 'After that business with Riverside, and the trial and everything, I just figured you were trying to get yourself into the set-up at Oldcester without me.'

'You weren't even interested! You wanted to come up here.'

'Oh, I guess I knew even then that I wouldn't make the grade. I'm good, but I'm not *that* good.'

Chris thought about this for a moment. 'Yes, you are,' he replied.

'Well, maybe I am,' said Nicky, smiling. 'But not without the right team, Chris. Not without you.'

Chris rubbed his hand across his face. His belly was rumbling softly. One chocolate bar wasn't going to keep him alive.

He knew he had to ask.

'OK. I accept everything you say, Nicky. We just got our wires crossed for a while. But under the bridge . . . you nearly killed me.'

'That's rubbish! You just rattled your head against that bollard!'

'If the bollard hadn't stopped me, I'd have fallen into the river!'

'If you'd fallen into the river, you would have got wet, not dead. I've seen you swim.'

'But I blacked out —'

'Oh, right, so if you'd hit your head on the bollard *and* fallen in the river, then you would have died? Yes, very likely. And even if it had happened, don't you think I would have tried to save you?'

'You pushed me!'

'You were chasing me!!'

'You were running away!!!'

Once again, they clammed up in unison, realising that they were getting rather loud. The priest/vicar/whatever had stopped and was looking all around him, trying to find out where the noise was coming from.

'We might as well go and let the Telfords catch us . . . it would save all this arguing.'

Chris laughed. Nicky was right. All this could wait for another day.

'Want to have a look?'

'Not yet,' replied Nicky. 'Let's leave it a bit longer.'

'We can't leave it too late. I've got a game tomorrow! I have to get back to Oldcester.'

'If the Telfords get hold of us, you'll go back in a box!'

'OK, OK. A few more minutes, then.'

They settled down to watch the gate. The guy in the cassock was walking that way himself. Perhaps he'd seen someone? The boys watched in silence.

The black-garbed man reached the gate, looked into the street outside, and then started to close one of the heavy portals.

'He's closing up!'

'Damn! This place must close at six!'

They leapt to their feet and pounded along the path towards the gate, yelling at him to wait. He looked round, obviously quite startled to see two boys racing towards him as if there were ghosts at their heels.

'Thanks!' called Chris as he went past the priest.

'Bye!' added Nicky, as he followed him through the gate.

They looked right and left, but there was no-one in sight. About 50 or 60 metres away, they could see a phone box.

'Let's go!' hissed Chris.

They raced to the box and grabbed at the receiver. Chris tipped change into the slot while Nicky dialled. Chris heard it ring, and an electronic clunk as it was picked up at the other end.

'Uncle Fabian? It's Nicky. Look, don't ask any questions, just come and pick me up. I'm in Bolton, near a cemetery. I don't know the name of the road. What? Yes, Chris is with me. Uh? OK, great! Hurry up!'

He put down the phone and turned. He was grinning with delight – but that faded quickly before Chris could ask anything. Nicky went white with horror.

Chris sensed a huge shadow fall over him from behind, making the area immediately around him as dark as if night had fallen. He turned, expecting to be looking into the piggy eyes of Barry Telford. Instead, he was looking at someone's chest. He tilted his head back and realised that though the face was just as porcine, it was bigger, and much higher in the air.

'Hi,' the new arrival said. 'I'm Les Telford. Barry's elder brother.'

Twenty-One

———— ⚽ ————

Next to his brother, Barry Telford looked like a scale model of what a proper Telford would look like. Les Telford was the complete article, with an expression that said that, unlike the prototype, he came with a working brain capable of working out complicated stuff like opening child-proof boxes.

The one thing you don't want to do here, Chris's brain was informing him, is make some clever wisecrack. That would not be a smart thing to do.

Meanwhile, his mouth was saying, 'Hi. Were you waiting to use the phone?'

Sadly, Les didn't look like the sort of bloke you had a laugh and a joke with. Not unless you were laughing about what you'd done to two kids outside a cemetery one Saturday. That would be funny.

Behind Les (well, behind and a bit to the side, actually – Chris couldn't see anything through Les's bulk), the smaller of the two pig-faced brothers was grinning. Perhaps he was already thinking about the stories they'd tell of the day they caught up with Nicky and his stupid mate with the clever mouth.

Les leaned closer, making Chris flinch. It was like being under a toppling wall.

'Very funny,' he said, grinning. Chris noticed he had an awful lot of fillings. 'You crack me up, you do. Why don't we go somewhere private and you can tell us some more funny stories?'

'Sorry,' said Chris, not sounding anything like as confident as his words. 'We've got to wait for someone.'

'Who were you phoning, Nicky?' barked Barry. Les didn't even twitch at the interruption. Chris tried hard not to look away.

'Chris is right. I called my uncle. He's coming to get us.'

'Is that so,' said Les, very slowly. 'Well, it's going to take him a while to get here from the estate, so we'll keep you company. Come on, I know a place where we can have a nice private chat.' He fixed his grip on Chris's shirt, almost pulling him off his feet. 'You want to come, don't you?' he asked, curling his lip.

'Desperately,' choked Chris.

About 400 metres along the road, over a railway bridge, there was a Victorian school building which was being torn down to make way for a brand new one, according to the sign fixed up over the old gate. The sign also warned parents of the dangers of children playing on building sites. 'They don't know the half of it,' Chris muttered to himself.

A steel fence had been erected around the site, but that was no obstacle to someone like Les Telford, who heaved one of the panels to one side. Chris noted that the end of the nearest terrace was still close enough for someone to hear them if they yelled loud enough.

Inside, they passed under a stone gate that had the word 'Girls' carved in the cornice, which amused the Telfords enormously as they pushed Chris and Nicky ahead. The building itself, which had once boasted two floors and a basement, was now an empty shell. The roof was gone and most of the upper floor had been knocked down, leaving half-windows in the brickwork like the spaces between ragged teeth.

The doors were all missing, so it was easy to push aside a sheet of rusty corrugated metal that had been put up in the place of one of them, and enter a short hallway. Inside, the glass and wood panels that divided the space into classrooms were all smashed, and the floor had been ripped up, exposing bare concrete.

A stone staircase in the corner of the building wound round in a tight spiral. They climbed up to the open second floor, feeling the coolness of the early evening air once more. The classrooms on this floor were even more wrecked. The Telfords led the boys into one, where all that remained to show the room's former purpose were a few painted cupboards and shelves and a battered old blackboard. Chris and

Nicky were dumped on the floor, facing the front of the class. Les prepared to teach them a lesson. Suddenly, double geography looked an awful lot better.

'You've cost us money today, Nicky,' he said, signalling to his brother. Barry brought the bag over.

Dipping inside, Les pulled out a fairly ordinary radio/cassette player, a camera, some boxes of film, a pair of jeans and three cheap digital watches, all still in their boxes or with price tags attached. He tutted.

'It's not much to show for a day's work, is it, Nicky? Not when you take into account that me and Barry paid your fare to get here —'

'Your fare,' echoed Barry, counting 'one' on his fingers.

'. . . Lunch.'

'Lunch,' repeated Barry, raising another finger. His brother glowered at him and Barry stood there, looking sheepish, with his hand showing two fingers to his brother.

'This load of old tat isn't worth much more than that. Very poor. Very poor indeed.' He dumped the gear back in the bag. Standing over by the outer wall, Barry had opened a packet of biscuits he had been carrying in his baggy brown coat, and was munching through them, jamming his mouth full, and chewing so slowly it appeared he had stopped breathing.

'That radio costs sixty-five quid,' said Nicky, defensively. He still looked pretty sick with anxiety. Increasingly, Chris knew why.

'Sixty-five quid in a shop, yeah,' explained Les, 'but we're going to be able to sell it for fifteen, maybe twenty. Half for us, half for you. 'That means you get less than a tenner. And you still owe us eighty.'

'I only borrowed fifty quid — and I've nicked loads of stuff for you!' Nicky protested, and then he looked at Chris sheepishly. Chris shook his head in despair. 'Well, not that much,' Nicky added.

Les ignored him. 'There's the interest and stuff,' he said, accounting for the difference. 'Expenses and that. Soon mounts up.'

'It's not fair,' Nicky complained, but he wasn't going to make much of an argument about it. Les Telford turned away and fastened up the bag, jiggling it to make sure the goods were all inside. He moved with exaggerated care, leaving the boys to stew.

Chris looked around at their bleak surroundings, trying to think how they were going to get out of this situation. He was sure the school wasn't a very safe place to be, and not just because the Telfords were clearly going to make their lives very uncomfortable in the next half hour. In places, the floor gaped open, the boards torn up or burned through. The outer wall was battered and one small column of bricks teetered perilously.

'You shouldn't have knocked off early today, Nicky,' Les sneered, and as Chris turned back he saw his eyes move from Nicky to Chris and back again. 'Or run us a dance around town.' The piggy eyes moved back. 'Nor involved your mate.'

'He's nothing to do with this,' Nicky cried. His voice dropped when Les glared at him. 'He doesn't owe you anything!'

'That's true,' nodded Les. 'Which means we don't need him. It means he's expandable.'

Chris choked out a sharp laugh at Les's mistake. The Telford brothers focused on him. 'Expandable means getting fat,' Chris explained, still chuckling. 'You mean expendable.'

'Well, thank you,' said Les, his face darkening. 'Expendable. That's you, then. Expendable.'

'Better than being expandable,' said Chris, 'like your brother.'

Barry howled angrily, clenching his fists. Les's eyes glittered like stars. He held up a hand to stay his brother's wrath.

'You really have got a very big mouth,' he informed Chris.

'But I don't fill it with food all the time,' replied Chris quickly. 'If I was as fat as your brother, I'd never be able to play football, see?'

A suspicious expression passed across Les's face. He clearly hadn't worked out what Chris was trying to achieve, but if the aim was to get him rattled, it wasn't going to succeed. Barry, on the other hand, was trying to swear and threaten Chris, which wasn't successful either, since all that happened was that he sprayed the room with half-chewed biscuit. Before Les could stop him, junior Pig-face had launched himself across the room and knocked Chris flat. He sat on Chris's chest, breathing hard and dribbling mushed biscuit on to his face.

'I'm going to hurt you real bad,' he said. Chris tried to shift him, but Barry didn't move an inch.

He heard someone walking closer across the creaking floorboards. Les Telford appeared from behind his brother, looking down on Chris with an amused smile on his face. He crouched down beside his brother and gripped Chris's chin in his fist.

'What was that meant to achieve?' he asked, and he delivered a ringing slap across Chris's cheek. 'Were you hoping you could distract us? Give yourself a chance to escape?'

It had sounded a lot better plan when Chris had cooked it up in his head than it did now.

'You little prat,' Les muttered. 'You're not going to escape.'

'What are you going to do with him?' gasped Nicky. Chris couldn't see Fiorentini from where he was lying under Barry's bulk. He hoped Nicky had a plan in mind that worked better than his had.

'Me? Nothing,' said the older Telford, and he stood up. Chris heard him walk behind his brother, then he reappeared on the other side, picking his way carefully over the ripped-up flooring and rubble, heading towards some junk heaped in the corner.

'So, you're a footballer as well, eh?' he said, as he picked through the rubbish. Several tins of empty and almost-empty school powder paint rolled across the floor, crashing noisily.

'That's right.'

'Just like Nicky-boy . . .'

'Only better,' said Chris. It was a pity he couldn't see Nicky's face. However, the noise the paint pots had made had given him the beginnings of an idea. If he could get hold of one and throw it out of the window, he might just be able to hit the outside of the terraced houses, or at least make it clatter along the street as it landed. With luck, someone would come out to tell whoever was in the school to pack it in.

'Really?' Les was speaking very slowly, clearly having trouble talking and searching at the same time. 'Did you hear that, Nicky? Your mate thinks he's pretty good. You used to think you were pretty good too, didn't you, Nicky? Only

152

Manchester United thought you were useless, and tossed you aside for me to find. You're on my team now, aren't you, Nicky?'

Chris heard Nicky mumble something.

Les turned, his face glowing with spite. 'What was that?' he asked.

'I said "yes",' Nicky replied quickly. Telford didn't look convinced. Chris wasn't so sure he would have been either.

Les went back to his search and finally he found what he was looking for. Crawling back out of the rubble, he turned and smacked a length of broken scaffolding into the palm of his left hand. It was perhaps a foot and a half in length, and one end was twisted and ragged.

Telford went back over to where his brother had Chris pinned.

'Take hold of his arms,' he said.

Barry lifted himself off Chris and moved round above his head. Chris stuggled to get up but Les lowered a boot on to his belly and held him down. Next moment, his wrists were locked in Barry's rough grip. This was starting to look a little ugly.

'What are you doing?' asked Nicky desperately.

Les threw the pipe into Nicky's lap, then dropped to his knees over Chris's ankles, pinning his feet just as securely as Barry had his hands. Chris could turn his waist and hips a little in each direction, but he couldn't really move much beyond that.

'Pick it up,' snarled Les, 'and come here.'

Nicky picked up the broken pole like he was on auto-pilot. He went round beside the older Telford, kneeling where he was told to. More and more, Chris felt a growing panic in his guts.

'Your mate is a bit too gobby for our liking,' said Les. 'I don't think he's very funny. What he needs is a lesson.' He used one hand to point at Chris's knee.

'He thinks he's better than you, Nicky. Well, you can soon settle that. Do his legs, Nicky-boy.'

Chris felt his whole body tense. He couldn't believe what he'd just heard. He could see how Nicky's face was hot and wet with fear. He knew he must look a lot worse.

'Les . . . I . . . I can't . . .' Nicky stammered.

'Course you can! One hit — WHAM!' He smashed his hand on the floor to emphasise his point. Nicky flinched as if he had been struck. 'That'll settle him, won't it? And you want to see him settled, don't you Nicky? You want to show him who really is the best?'

'But . . . I . . . I just . . . can't . . .'

Having tried to encourage Nicky to go along with his plan, Les quickly fell back on his more natural talent of threatening him instead. Of the two, Chris knew which he felt Nicky would be more likely to cave in under.

'You owe me money, Nicky . . .' Les was explaining slowly. 'That means I own you! Do it!!! DO IT!!!'

'Look,' said Chris quickly, 'if it's money you want, I can get it! I'm up here to talk to Manchester United. If I sign for them, my agent says he can get me twenty thousand quid.' He raised his voice, trying to get Les to look at him. So far, he hadn't removed his glaring eyes from Nicky by so much as a fraction. Chris knew that in five seconds his dreams of playing football could be over for ever. 'Twenty grand, Telford. It's yours, if you let me go!'

'Twenty thousand quid,' repeated Telford. 'Did you once tell me that some bloke was going to pay you ten grand, Nicky? That's only half as much.' He grinned, cruelly confident of his power. 'Maybe he is better than you, Nicky.'

'He isn't!' Nicky insisted, his voice high with strain.

'That isn't how it sounds to me. It sounds to me like you got blown out, and your mate is going to get all your money.'

Nicky turned his head fractionally and looked at Chris.

Chris had never seen anyone look at him with so much undisguised pain and hatred before. He saw Nicky's hand tighten on the metal pipe.

'Do him,' whispered Les, and he leaned forward once more to point at Chris's knee. 'Do his legs . . .'

Chris screamed as Nicky drew back his arm, and the pipe whistled through the air. There was a sickening, ringing thump. Chris felt a brief, searing pain in his leg . . .

Les Telford toppled forwards, still wearing the same sadistic smile. His eyes, though, had become very glassy. He smashed on to the floor at Chris's side, his belt buckle tearing at Chris's leg as he hit the floor.

154

'Les!!!' yelled Barry, and Chris saw Nicky's eyes widen as the younger Telford launched himself at him. He tried to fend him off with the pipe but it bounced off his attacker's shoulder and he lost his grip. The pipe spun off somewhere towards the back of the classroom.

Barry flattened Nicky to the floor and raised his fists as if to pound his head through the floor. Chris had only a half-second to react. He rolled over, grabbed at the thug's arm, and held it back.

'Run, Nicky!' he yelled.

Nicky jumped to his feet. Chris tried to see how he was going to be able to escape as well, but he knew he didn't have a hope. Barry Telford reached round, grabbed his shirt front and dragged him round in front.

Chris didn't even see the blow that hit him coming. Barry had cuffed him with the back of his hand, smacking him in the lip. He tasted blood.

It took him a moment to pull his senses together. Nicky was racing for the door and Barry was looking to cut him off. It was a race Nicky was going to win. Showing sense for the first time, Telford gave up the chase and turned back to make certain of the easier target. Chris scrambled to his feet.

He considered diving for the window, but that would be suicide. Of course, it looked like standing still while Barry Telford ran him over wouldn't be too healthy either.

Chris braced himself for the impact, but it never came. Suddenly Telford was stumbling, flying through the air with a look of stunned bewilderment on his face. Nicky had tripped him from behind. Chris threw himself to one side and felt rather than saw the thug land. There was a huge, rending crash and a vast plume of dust. As it cleared, Chris realised Barry had gone clean through the floor.

He was lying on the edge of the gap himself. Down below, Telford was lying on a pile of plaster, wood and hardboard. He was breathing, but he wasn't going anywhere.

'Told you you needed to diet . . .' muttered Chris.

He rolled painfully away from the hole and looked up. The clouds of smoke were still thick; a grey smog mixed with twists of red and yellow from the powder paint. Chris waited for it to clear.

Slowly, he realised he could see a shadow that had to be Nicky.

'That was a professional foul,' he coughed. He heard Nicky laugh in return.

'I'm glad you went for the right target,' Chris said. He remembered that awful moment when he hadn't known if Nicky would bring the pipe down on his leg or Les's head. It made him cold to think about it.

'You were winding me up,' he heard Nicky say from the cloud.

'I thought you might need a bit of help,' said Chris. 'Trouble was, when I told Les I was getting twenty grand from United, I wondered if you might break my legs after all.'

'I thought about it, but then I thought "twenty grand"? He's saying some agent thinks he's worth twice as much as me? That's when I knew you were lying.'

Chris laughed as well, and lay his head back on the floorboards. After a moment, he looked up and saw that the dusty, multi-coloured fog was slowly settling. Nicky's outline was becoming steadily clearer . . .

Which was when Chris realised Fiorentini's wasn't the only shadow he could see.

Les Telford emerged from the murk, his face ghostly pale, marked with a darkening bruise on one temple. His hands were outstretched, reaching for Nicky's throat.

Nicky was kneeling, hands on his thighs, recovering his breath. He had no idea that disaster was about to grab him from behind.

Chris shouted a warning, but he knew it would be too late. There was nothing he could do to stop –

One of the tins of powder paint lay at Chris's feet. He was on his side, facing Nicky, and the tin was by the toe of his left shoe, sitting up very slightly on a patch of plaster. The idea flew into his head and he snatched at it.

Still half-sprawled on the floor, Chris snapped back his right foot and let fly. He caught the tin with his instep and it took off like a rocket. Les Telford had time to do no more than open his eyes wide in horror as the pot flew at his face from out of the gloom.

The tin bounced off the elder Pig-face's head with a dull

bong. Some of the paint at the bottom had hardened to the consistency of granite, and the tin had the weight of Chris's boot behind it too. Better yet, though, there was still some loose powder inside as well. As it struck, a cloud of green powder paint exploded over Telford's face.

Les uttered a gagging yell of pain and staggered back against a battered old table. The creaky furniture made a small groan of protest, and then decided to go out on strike. As Telford hit the ground, shards of wood and more clouds of dust flew up all round him.

'Let's get out of here!' Chris screamed at Nicky, racing towards the door.

Nicky's jaw was gaping wide enough to do himself an injury, but he caught on fast and they flew out of the classroom as fast as their feet could fly.

As they reached the ground floor, they could hear Barry stirring on the pile of debris he had landed on. 'We'll get you! We'll bloody get you!' he screeched as he saw them race by.

'BARRY!' came a thunderous roar.

'Coming, Les!' he wailed.

Chris and Nicky didn't wait to see what help he could give his brother. They chased along the hall, aiming for the door. Moments later, they were out in the playground.

Chris kicked open the fencing as they reached it and they went out into the street. The light was fading fast and a few dirty-orange street lamps were slowly coming to life. They looked left and right. There was a car in the distance to the right, but there was nowhere to hide if they ran that way and the car didn't stop.

Left, then. They took off together, racing over the railway bridge. Ahead of them, the street stretched off towards the cemetery. Too many dead-ends; nowhere to hide.

Chris glanced back. There was no sign of the Telfords, although he fancied he could hear the scraping of the metal door being bent back.

'Down here!' he yelped at Nicky, turning around the wall at the end of the bridge and through a broken fence.

The ground fell away sharply into a deep cutting. A railway line stretched off one way, in deep shadow. Underneath where they were scrambling down, the tunnel opened like a pitch-black mouth.

'We're heading back towards them!' hissed Nicky.

'We can't out-run them!' said Chris, bouncing off a lump of exposed earth as he tumbled through the weeds and stringy grass. 'We've got to double back, throw them off the scent.'

They hit the bottom, Nicky close behind Chris. They could hear shouts and hard-soled footsteps in the street above.

'In here!' breathed Chris urgently, pulling at Nicky's arm. They ducked into the unlit tunnel. Chris felt a clutch of fear in his guts as they were swallowed up in the blackness. Railway bridges had ceased to be his favourite places long ago.

It wasn't a wide bridge and there was just enough light at the far end to guide them. They stepped quickly across the sleepers, crossing to the far side. No sound penetrated the gloomy darkness.

'Think they'll head straight on?' asked Nicky.

'I hope so,' whispered Chris.

That hope was soon shattered. A ragged, brutal voice called at them from behind. They looked back and saw the Telford brothers were framed in brutal silhouette against the light of the tunnel mouth.

'They've seen us!' shrieked Nicky. 'What now?'

'I don't know,' admitted Chris, standing perfectly still and watching as the Telfords started to move towards them. They seemed so close and – somehow – their outlines seemed to be getting sharper and the light around them even brighter . . .

'Run!' yelled Chris, and a second later an urgent, wailing horn sounded. The Telfords turned, saw the approaching lights of the train, and Chris could just about hear their screams as they flung themselves back out of the tunnel. He looked away, knowing that he and Nicky were no safer at their end of the tunnel. He pulled Nicky hurriedly towards the embankment as the train hurried through, deafening them with the sound of its horn, the squealing of its brakes and the thunderous roar of the wind as it swept past.

They dragged themselves up the embankment as quickly as they could, but the fright had drained them. Long before they reached the top, Les Telford was at the bottom, climbing rapidly up behind them. His face was twisted with venomous rage, while sweat was streaking the ghoulish green paint. Chris had no doubt that, if he caught them, Les was going to make them pay dearly for what they had put him through.

They reached the top scant metres ahead of him. A little more of their lead was lost crawling under the mesh fence. They turned on to the bridge and tried to find their legs again, but they were drained of strength by their fear. As they passed the centre of the bridge, where a car was parked by the kerb, they could feel Les Telford's hands reaching out to snatch them.

A car . . .

Chris turned, knowing that the car hadn't been there when they crossed the bridge before, recognising what it was even as he saw the door swing open into Telford's legs. With a piercing scream, the bully was dashed to the ground against the bridge wall.

The door opened wider and Uncle Fabian looked out, his face a mixture of concern and relief. 'Here you are!' he sighed, as if he had lost sight of them for ten minutes.

Nicky fell into his uncle's arms and then quickly opened the Mercedes' back door and dived inside. Chris started to follow. He looked at Les Telford, clutching his leg on the pavement, cursing and groaning, and then he saw Barry a few metres away, clutching the bag of stolen goods, looking at him as if he had just been plucked from the bridge by an alien spacecraft.

Chris closed the gap on him in a few strides.

'Give me the bag,' he said, his voice full of steel. He looked up at his opponent and felt Barry's will break. Junior Pig-face, looking sheepish, handed the bag over.

Chris threw it on to the back seat of the car and followed it in.

'You still owe us, Fiorentini!' snarled Les.

'And you owe me for denting my door,' said Uncle Fabian, pulling it closed. He let the electric window down. 'Want to call it even, sonny?'

Les didn't answer. Uncle Fabian shrugged and smiled broadly. Slipping the shift into drive, he pulled away from the bridge, leaving the Telfords rapidly and finally behind.

159

Twenty-Two

An hour into the game, Iain Walsh pulled Chris off. Since half-time, his striker had been reduced to a crawl, and even as he trotted off the pitch it was clear he was almost hobbling.

'You OK?' asked Walsh.

'Just some stiffness,' replied Chris, easing off his boots and stretching his aching limbs. He'd had an attack of cramp just after half-time. 'I was hoping it would run off but it didn't.'

Too much running, that was the problem, thought Chris, sighing. After chasing all over Bolton the day before, not to mention almost getting smeared by the Telfords, Chris was exhausted. It had been a real effort to drag himself out of bed in time for the game! Still, the Colts were 2–0 up and the opposition didn't look like they had much more to offer.

Walsh didn't press the point but went off along the touchline, reorganising the team to its new shape. So long as he had played his part in the win – and Chris had scored the first goal – Walsh wasn't going to mind too much if Chris was a little off-par.

Not everyone was going to be so patient, though. Chris had just laid back on the grass, closing his eyes and yawning, when he felt a shadow fall over him and an impatient voice called his name.

'Hi, Sean,' he said, sitting up.

Priest was wearing a deep frown and had his hands folded across his chest. Just behind him, Ray Foulds had also turned up to see the second half, and he looked equally concerned.

'What's the matter with you today?' asked Priest. Chris decided not to mention that he'd scored the first goal while Sean hadn't been there to see. He knew his second half

160

performance had been pretty lame, and in Sean's book you played for 90 minutes or not at all.

'Cramp. I've probably been overdoing it a bit,' Chris explained, although it didn't even sound convincing to him.

'Looks more like you're half-asleep to me,' Priest snapped. 'What time did you get to bed last night?'

Quickly considering the truth – which was that Uncle Fabian had dropped him off at about 1am – Chris elected for a little creative evasion.

'Late.'

Unsurprisingly, Priest didn't look satisfied with that reply. 'I thought I told you that I didn't want you staying up all hours on Saturdays when we have a morning kick-off?'

'I had a small crisis to look after,' said Chris.

'What sort of crisis?' demanded Priest, who clearly wasn't going to be fobbed off easily.

'One with a happy ending,' replied Chris quickly.

Priest looked intrigued but doubtful. 'Go on,' he said.

'You remember Nicky Fiorentini?' Chris asked. Priest nodded. 'What would you say if I said we could get him to play for us?'

To Chris's disappointment, Priest didn't immediately look as if he was going to forgive Chris for his weak performance in the game. 'I thought he was in Manchester?' he said.

'Not any more,' Chris replied, trying to sound as if he thought this was the best news since sliced bread.

'Uh-huh . . .' said Priest.

'He came home yesterday. The Manchester thing didn't work out. That means he'll be back at Spirebrook, and he's available to play for the Colts too.' Priest didn't reply, and Chris realised he was thinking about what he'd been told. 'You said I should tell you if there were any other players at Spirebrook who were worth looking at; well, now there is. You've seen Nicky; you know he can play.' Still Priest didn't say anything. Chris found himself getting quite heated with him. 'Look,' he said. 'Nicky and I are a team. We work well together. You might not have seen the best of him, but I promise you that it's true. That day at the trial, well, Nicky was just upset about a few things, and it affected his game. If you don't believe me, ask Mr Foulds.'

161

He switched his attention from the Oldcester Youth Team boss to the scout, looking for his support. There had been a time when Chris had thought Foulds rated Nicky as a better player than him, and it had annoyed him greatly. He had spent six months proving that it wasn't true. But now it was almost what he wanted to hear.

When he looked at Foulds, however, he saw the older man had a very strange expression on his face. It wasn't a smile, it wasn't a frown, it wasn't sorrow or anger. It was unreadable.

'Tell him, Mr Foulds. Remember what you told us, when we first met you, about how we overlapped? About how having both of us together was better than us being separated?'

'I did say that,' said Foulds, and Chris faced Priest with a look that was supposed to say 'told you so' but which quickly faded into amazement as Foulds continued. 'It used to be true, Chris, but I don't think it is anymore. You've changed a lot in the last half year. You're a different player now.'

Chris couldn't believe what he was hearing. From the moment that Uncle Fabian's Mercedes had pulled away from the kerb on the railway bridge, Chris had felt as if his life had finally got back on track. They'd gone back to Aunt Clara's house to pick up Nicky's stuff. Uncle Fabian had written a cheque for her to post to the store from where Nicky had nicked the stuff, and promised her that he and his sons would be back if the Telfords gave her any trouble.

After that, they'd turned back for Oldcester. They'd stopped at some motorway services on the way, almost stripping the restaurant bare as they ate everything in sight. They swapped news; Chris told Nicky about what was happening at Spirebrook, and how things were set up at Riverside; Nicky told Chris all the good things that he'd seen in his brief stint as a United hopeful.

By the time they'd got back to Oldcester, everyone was exhausted, not least Uncle Fabian, who had listened to it all. His only part in the conversation was to tell the boys how he had found them. When Nicky had called his car phone, he had only been five minutes away. Amy Baxter and her posse had told Clara where Chris and Nicky might be found, and Uncle Fabian had been looking for them from about 4pm, after he had given up on his fruitless search around Old Trafford.

It took him a while to find the cemetery, and by then it was closed. Looking round, he'd seen four boys walking over the railway bridge, so he'd turned the car round to follow them, thinking that he had recognised Nicky. In the dark it was hard to tell.

By the time he reached the bridge, though, they'd disappeared. 'That must have been while we were in the school,' Nicky had deduced.

Uncle Fabian had driven right by them then, and gone to the far end of the road. He'd stopped there for a while and wandered over to a corner shop to ask if anyone in there had seen anything, after which he'd turned the car round and come back. He saw two boys come racing out of the school, rush over the bridge and disappear. This time, he'd been sure it was Chris and Nicky, and he knew they were in trouble when he saw the two bigger boys thundering after them.

'Particularly the one with the green face. He looked very mean.'

He had parked on the other side of the road, and was just getting ready to get out and look over the bridge when he heard the train rush past. It had frozen him with fear – he'd been terrified that they might have been in its path. Next moment, Chris and Nicky had appeared, running along the pavement towards his car, and they knew the rest of the story as well as he did.

Looking back, Chris knew that he would remember that episode for as long as he lived. Every detail was etched on his mind.

And, as a result, Nicky was back in Oldcester and the killer partnership could take up where it had left off. Or, at least, that's what he had thought, before coming face to face with Foulds' mysterious expression and Priest's complete lack of interest.

'What are you saying?' he asked the scout.

'All I'm saying,' said Foulds, 'is that it isn't so important to have the two of you together any more. You're a perfectly good player, even without Nicky to supply you.'

Chris was still reeling from that idea when Priest hit him with another.

'Apart from anything else,' the younger man said, running his hand through his thatch of corn-yellow hair, 'I'm not sure how Nicky would fit in with the Colts. Iain has already got you playing wide up front, alongside Rory Blackstone. He's got Jazz, Stamp, Polly and Basford across the middle. I don't see where Nicky is better than any of them. If he was going to get a place, Chris, it would be yours, but frankly I'd sooner have your goalscoring ability in this team than Nicky's skills on the wing any day.'

Chris really was staggered now. Priest was saying that Nicky wasn't *good* enough to play for the Colts?

'Just think about it, Chris. I'll speak to Iain but I'm sure he'll see things the same way I do. We need a bit more cover at the back, sure, but otherwise this team is shaping up just right. If I was honest, I'd tell you that we're not even trying that hard to find another goalkeeper.'

'Poor old Mac,' sighed Foulds.

Priest laughed. 'He's a good lad and a fair keeper. If he does grow a bit over the next few years, everything he's learned now will be worth its weight in gold.'

'I can't believe you don't want Nicky for the Colts!' cried Chris, still not satisfied that he understood.

'Next year might be different,' started Priest, 'and I'm sure Iain would be happy to have a proper look at him in the meantime.'

'Well, actually –' Now what? thought Chris, as he turned to face Foulds. It appeared that the mystery was about to be solved. 'He's already registered with another team.'

If Chris could have found a nice heavy rock at that moment, he would have happily sat pounding it against his head for half an hour until the pain went away. This really was becoming like some kind of bad dream.

'That was quick,' said Priest.

Foulds looked shifty for a moment, then decided to confess. 'Actually, his uncle called me this morning; asked me if I knew any of the Youth League teams who might be looking for a winger. As it happens, I did, and if all goes to plan I've got him fixed up with a team. He checked his watch. 'He should be seeing them now. If he's happy, he might be able to start playing for them next week.'

'Ignoring everything I just said,' Sean Priest remarked, scratching his chin, 'did you call Iain?'

'No.'

'For any particular reason?'

'Actually, I was of the same opinion as you, that Nicky wouldn't fit into the way the Colts play. You need midfield players like Jazz, people who can support the front two and get some goals themselves. If you had Nicky out wide up front, you couldn't afford to have both Rory and Chris.'

Priest nodded, almost satisfied. 'Is that the only reason?' he asked.

Foulds still looked uncomfortable. Chris wondered how on earth there could be anything left. 'Also, Nicky said he wanted to play for another team.' As Foulds said that, his eyes flicked at Chris.

As he had listened to the two men, Chris had slowly pulled himself to his feet and was watching them closely. Inside his guts, a seething, burning flare was building. This wasn't the kind of anger he had felt when Nicky had been behaving so erratically eight or nine months before, nor the kind of flash of instant temper he had allowed to get him into trouble against the lads from Blackmoor. This was different. Chris felt humiliated; betrayed.

'What is his problem?!!!' he yelled, directing the question at the sky.

'Chris?' Priest sounded worried.

'After all I went through to save his stupid neck up in Bolton. After all I went through before he left!' He threw his boots at the dressing room steps, then went storming after them. Foulds caught up with him just before he went through the door without opening it first.

'Wait a minute, son . . .'

Chris rounded on him, red-faced and hot with hostility. At that moment he realised that if Foulds had never come along to see them play, he and Nicky wouldn't be enemies now. It was like he'd taken an electric shock. 'I'm not your son! Stop treating me like you know me – you don't!! You don't know half what has happened in the last year!'

'Maybe not, but –'

'And now this!' Chris continued. 'I went up to Bolton; do

you really think I wanted to? I had to listen to music from the Stone Age; I nearly got myself killed by some green-faced imbecile and his brother, the biscuit-man; I nearly got myself killed by a train! And for what?'

'Chris, you're not making any sense . . .'

He reached out to stop Chris, fearing that he might just do himself an injury. Chris was like a coiled spring, ready to lash out in any direction.

'I thought we could put it all behind us. Get the old partnership back together again, just as it was before. Well, I was wrong. I was stupid! Damn it! And damn him!!!'

Chris broke free of Foulds' restraining hand and crashed through the door (which just about managed to open fast enough) into the changing rooms. The scout let him go.

Chris slipped out through a window, and he was long gone before Foulds thought to check inside.

'I thought this fight between Chris and Nicky was supposed to be a big secret,' observed Priest, after they'd finished searching for Chris and realised that he was gone.

'That's what Chris's father told me.'

Priest laughed dryly. 'Well, at least we don't have to pretend any more. Do you want a lift back into town?'

'Thanks,' said Foulds.

They walked round to where Priest had parked his car. He fished his keys from his pocket, unlocked the car and opened the driver's door. Then he paused, one foot on the door sill.

'So, who has Nicky registered to play with?'

'Gainsbury Town's youth team.'

Priest's eyebrows arched – and he whistled through the wide 'O' made by his lips. 'We play them next Sunday!'

'I know,' said Foulds, climbing into the passenger seat.

Priest went to say something, then thought better of it. He grinned widely. 'Should be an interesting game,' he said to himself.

Chris was marginally less furious by the time he got to Nicky's house, but only in the sense that the fire thrown by a volcano is cooler than the surface of the sun. He was still pretty hot.

Nicky wasn't there. In fact, only grandma and one of the daughters were in the Fiorentini house, and since the old lady only spoke Italian (and only that when she realised someone was talking to her), Chris had tried to take his temper out on a ten-year-old girl who didn't have a clue what was going on, and who looked as if she might burst into tears if Chris so much as raised his voice.

'Nicky's gone to London, with Uncle Fabian and my cousin Luke,' she explained.

'Oh! Gone to try his luck with Spurs, has he?' commented Chris sarcastically. It was wasted on Luciana, who was probably the only Fiorentini who had no interest in football.

'Sorry?'

'Never mind. So when will he be back?'

'I'm not sure. Next weekend, I think.'

'Next weekend? What about school?'

'Oh, he's not going to school this week!' Her face had developed a sulky pout. 'Everyone says he deserves a break, after what he's been through. I never get a day off school –'

'After what he's been through?' gasped Chris, cutting Luciana off before she could feel too sorry for herself.

'That's what I said,' agreed Luciana.

'Great. I don't suppose he told you anything about the football team he went to see this morning?'

'Oh, he had plenty to say – as usual! He said they wanted him, and that he'd play for them next week if he could. There was a lot of talk about forms that had to be filled in, or something. My father's taking them to some man in –'

'What was their name?'

'Whose?'

'The team Nicky is going to play for!'

Luciana shrugged. She would never be likely to remember something like that. Chris figured that was about all he could accomplish here. Suddenly Luciana's eyes lit up, as a thought bubbled to the surface. 'Oh! He told me to give you a message, though.'

'Really? What is it?'

'See you next Sunday.'

Chris tried hard to work out what that might mean. Where

would he be likely to run into Nicky on Sunday? After he'd played for Riverside Colts at Gainsbury, Chris was supposed to be finishing his homework, and then he and his father were going to work on converting the old box room into a study, with a built-in desk, shelves and space for a computer.

Was Nicky just going to pop round on the off-chance that he'd be home? It didn't sound likely.

The truth overwhelmed Chris, like a freak wave coming ashore. He staggered under the sheer stupidity of it all. Surely, Nicky couldn't have –

'This team . . . it wasn't called Gainsbury, was it?'

Luciana's face lit up again, and Chris moaned in agony as her face confirmed what he had already guessed. 'That's it!' she was crying as he turned away. 'Nicky's very excited, Chris. Apparently they've got quite an important game next week.'

Twenty-Three

Gainsbury was a small town on the edge of Oldcester, a place of smart houses and an old shopping street that had been swallowed up by the city and transformed into a suburb. The centre of town was dominated by an old church and by the narrow streets of the original village, but a smart 'new' road had been opened up along the west side of the town in the 1950s, which had attracted new businesses and housing. Eventually, the road connected Blackmoor and the rest of south Oldcester with the M49.

Right beside this busy route, sandwiched between a B&Q superstore and a carpet warehouse which had year-round sales and 'unrepeatable' offers, Gainsbury Town's rickety old stadium was home to a Beazer Homes League side, a 'B' team which played in the County League, and several junior sides. The official youth team had been part of the Oldcester Youth League since before the war, and some of the kids playing for them now were the sons and grandsons of previous players.

Two players stuck out like sore thumbs among the keen but basically very ordinary players kitted out in Gainsbury's all white. One was a blond-haired tough with an unpleasant scowl on his face and a split lip which had swollen to the size and colour of a fat grape.

The other had black hair, an impish grin, and a bruised eye that was more than a little swollen. Chris watched them both as the two teams went through their warm-ups. The bully from Blackmoor and Nicky Fiorentini. Now, what little escapade had they been through together?

Chris and the rest of the Riverside team stretched out their limbs and practised passing drills around the penalty box. Jazz

169

kept looking into the other half, missing the ball and causing Iain Walsh to yell angrily at him. Chris ran over and slapped Javinder on the back.

'Keep your mind on the game, Jazz,' he hissed.

'But it's Nicky!' Javinder said, his mouth wide with wonderment. 'What's he doing playing for the other side?'

'You can find out later,' urged Chris, whipping a quick pass to the other boy's feet. Jazz managed to trap it and flick it back roughly in Chris's direction. 'First we beat them, then we find out what's been going on, OK?'

Chris left Jazz still gaping in amazement into the other half, and went off to find Riverside's left back, Mike Tollie. If Chris felt sorry for anyone this afternoon, it was Mike. He was a decent defender, who liked to get forward himself when he could. This afternoon he was going to have his hands full with Nicky.

'He'll try and fake you out whenever he can,' he reminded Tollie. 'He's got a really deceptive body swerve. He'll try and bluff you into committing yourself in the tackle, then he'll take it round you.'

Tollie nodded nervously. The dressing room had been full of rumour about Gainsbury's new signing. The year before, the two teams had drawn 1–1 in the same fixture; several of the old hands were of the opinion that this would be one of the hardest games of the season, even more so now that Gainsbury had bolstered their defence and picked up some quicksilver on the wing. The others had quizzed Chris, Mac and Jazz about rumours they'd heard about Nicky, which made him sound as if he was Giggs or Kanchelskis.

'What you have to remember is that he wants to go outside you. Nicky loves space, and if you can force him inside, you can get some support from the others. Sometimes, he'll try to make you think he wants to come inside: don't fall for it. Just show him the inside, and make him run towards the rest of the defenders.'

'What about if he has a clear run at goal?' asked Tollie.

Chris sighed. 'Look, obviously there are going to be times when you're just going to have to take him on in the best way you can. What I'm saying is, if you can, make him come inside rather than let him go round you.'

170

'Or you could just clatter him,' observed Jackson, unhelpfully.

'Try that round our penalty area, and you'll get to find out how good he is at free kicks,' said Chris, gesturing at Jackson to back off. He tried one last piece of advice. 'It's better to slow him down than try and tackle him. He's quick, and he doesn't like it when defenders won't try and beat him at his own game. If you slow him down —'

'All right, all right,' said Tollie. 'It's only a Gainsbury player, Chris. It's not Ryan Giggs.'

Chris decided against telling him who Nicky had trained with once.

Having sorted out who would be marking Nicky, Chris stepped up to the halfway line to see if he could work out how the defence would line up from the way they were warming up. The left back was a slow, one-footed player who seemed to find it hard to judge the pace of his passes. One of the centre backs was easier to sum up.

'Hey!' called Chris.

The lad from Blackmoor eventually realised that Chris was calling him. His face took on a dark colour as he jogged half-heartedly towards the centre.

'What do you want?'

'I owe you an apology,' Chris told him. The blond defender looked at Chris suspiciously. 'I was supposed to be at Loam Park, Saturday before last. You remember? Two o'clock? You were going to show me how hard you were without your mates?'

'Yeah,' said the boy, his face briefly arrogant and hostile. 'You bottled. I waited.'

Chris tutted. 'Sorry. Didn't mean to be unreliable. I got caught up in something else. Next week do you instead?'

The other boy — Bennett, Chris suddenly remembered — got that hard, icy glint in his eye, but said nothing. Finally, he shook his head. 'Forget it,' he said.

Chris was secretly delighted. Even so, he was more than a little curious as to what had changed his opponent's mind. 'You sure? I mean, if it's because of that split lip your kid sister's given you —'

Once again, the other lad seemed to be on the point of

171

accepting Chris's challenge. Slowly, though, he calmed down. 'I said it's sorted.'

Chris waited, hoping he might say more, but the Blackmoor tough wasn't going to give him any more.

'Good,' said Chris at once, relaxing his stance. 'I'd rather play football.' He stuck out his hand.

Bennett eyed it for a moment. 'We're supposed to do that at the end,' he said. Then he reached out and they shook hands once.

That buried one part of the past. Chris stepped back and jogged away backwards, hearing the ref call the two teams to be ready for the kick-off.

'I'm still going to make a monkey out of you this afternoon,' he laughed. The other boy grinned back and did a passable ape impersonation.

'What are you doing?' asked Rory as Chris joined his team mate.

'Just sizing up the opposition,' said Chris, and he waited for the whistle to start a game that he hoped would settle a few more old scores.

In the haphazard old wooden stand, two dozen spectators clapped their hands, called on favoured players to 'come on' and stamped their feet to ward off the first chilly Sunday of autumn. The ref blew his whistle and waved the two teams into action. Chris bit his lip, then fixed his concentration on the next 90 minutes and moved into Gainsbury's half.

There are games where, almost from the minute the first kick-off is taken, you know you are going to see two average teams, out of form, plod through 90 minutes of tedious, poor-quality football, ending up with the same number of goals as when they started. You find yourself watching them on TV, giving them just another five minutes to make *something* happen. It never does, and you realise you watched it to the end simply because you couldn't believe football could be that bad.

There are games where one team plays well, showing a little creativity, a little flair and ambition, but every neutral in the ground knows that it will be the boring, defensive, organised team who will score the only goal on the break, having managed nothing more constructive than an endless sequence of offside traps.

But, the gods of football be thanked, there are other games. Games where two teams come together in the mood to do something spectacular. Everything happens to within a centimetre of perfection; runs are timed just right to evade the defence, passes land perfectly for team mates to run on to, tackles arrive at the last second, whisking the ball away just as the striker is getting ready to fire the ball into the net.

That early October Sunday, with the sun angling through low cloud and illuminating the pitch with a cool, yellow-white light, two dozen parents, friends, passers-by and dogs watched Gainsbury Tigers and Riverside Colts play a match that was better than 90 per cent of the fare served up by that summer's European Championship. There should have been cameras, there should have been commentators, and there should have been a ring of photographers round each goal (and they should have had plenty of film). Instead, one parent recorded about fifteen minutes of the game on videotape, and then stopped recording because he just wanted to watch.

Gainsbury played out of their skins. Something had galvanised them, made them want to fight for every ball. Their midfield tackled hard, chased down on the man in possession, raced after the loose ball. They didn't have the Colts' eye for the game or skill on the ball, but they made the midfield a battleground.

For all the competitiveness, the quality of passing that came out of midfield on both sides was startling. Chris and Rory on one side, and the Tigers' strikers on the other, were able to feast on a rich diet of quality ball.

It could have been a nightmare for the defenders, but they too played their part in a brilliant game. In the second minute, Chris watched in amazement as the guy from Blackmoor threw himself along the goal-line to head clear a shot that had look destined to hit the back of the net. At the other end, Nicky curled a cross into the box, and the taller of the Gainsbury strikers met it perfectly with the centre of his forehead, cracking the ball just under the bar. Somehow, Mac

– judging the moment to perfection – catapulted himself off the ground to touch the ball over. Everyone in the ground gasped.

Everyone was playing better than they had ever played, better than they knew how to play. Ordinary players were transformed into rough diamonds; OK players were made to look like stars. Two players, though, still outshone them all.

Nicky's touch on the ball was magical. His passes from midfield were flat, fast and outstandingly accurate. More often than he passed, though, he looked to take Tollie on. His ball control was uncanny; sometimes it would seem that he had let it slip away, and then he would snake out his foot and just touch the ball away from a tackle, hurdling the defender's outstretched leg as he chased after it. He turned this way and that, wriggling like a snake. He never seemed to turn the way anyone expected.

Tollie could have been made to look stupid, but he fought hard and made himself difficult to beat by retreating in front of Nicky, slowing the winger down. He launched tackles only when he had a good sight at the ball. Several times, he broke up Gainsbury's attacks on his own.

Every now and again, though, Nicky would be too clever for him. As Chris had feared, Nicky bluffed Tollie repeatedly, shaping up to go one way and then turning the other, leaving the defender stranded.

Once he got clear, Nicky turned on the burners and sprinted away with the ball, leaving the other defenders to try and cover the hole he had made. Nicky tried one rasping shot himself, which bent away past the post. Twelve minutes into the game, though, he hit a diagonal ball across the box, which evaded three defenders by fractions of an inch, and the Gainsbury centre forward was left with a close-range tap-in.

Chris watched the goal from just inside his own half. It was the sort of goal Nicky had provided him with dozens of times. Shaking his head, Chris lined up for the restart.

'Nicky's on form,' said Javinder, from a few metres behind.

Chris turned to face him. He felt a dull, angry pain in his guts. 'He's using this like an exhibition game, just to remind us what he can do.' He gritted his teeth. 'This is all about Nicky making himself look better than us, to remind us how much we need him. Well, he isn't, and we don't. Come on, Jazz, let's show him what we can do!'

It took all of three minutes for them to do just that. Javinder collected the ball from Mac's kick, beat a man in midfield, and moved up through the centre. His change of gear took him into space, and two Gainsbury defenders moved up quickly to try and close him down.

Before they could get too close, Jazz flicked the ball forward off his instep towards Rory Blackstone. Rory was tightly marked, but the pass was so accurate that he was able to lay it back to Jazz, who ran on to the return pass and took it in his stride. Gainsbury were all over the place, and the last defender and the keeper rushed out in a desperate bid to block Jazz's route to goal.

Neither of them got within three metres of him before he cut the ball across the box to where Chris had ghosted into the box. He wasn't just unmarked – no-one had even noticed him. It was a formality to bury the ball into the back of the net.

'That was a beauty!' laughed Rory, and Jazz looked equally delighted.

'That was your goal,' said Chris, slapping the midfielder's palms. Then, without thinking, he bopped his head against Javinder's brow.

'OW!!!' yelled Jazz. Chris jumped back in surprise. He and Nicky had banged heads after a goal like that – but Jazz hadn't been ready.

'Jeez – sorry, mate! You all right?'

Javinder felt his nose gingerly. 'I think so . . . God, Chris – how do you celebrate a hat-trick; shooting people?'

Chris apologised again.

'Better not try that with me!' declared Rory.

'He'd need a stepladder . . .' muttered Jazz, grinning.

The first half continued at much the same blistering pace. Rory slammed a header in from about ten metres; Nicky set up a move in midfield that saw Gainsbury catch the Colts' defence lying a little flat and Mac beaten from close in. Two-two.

Then, after Mac had pulled off a brilliant save from a Nicky free kick, Chris picked up the ball just outside his own box and sprinted out, going wide along the right. His impression of Nicky even included going round the full back, and then he sent over a hanging cross which Rory climbed up for, thumping the ball goal-bound with his head. The keeper pushed the ball on to the bar, but Adam Parker cracked in the rebound.

Finally, just before half-time, Nicky laid off the ball with an outrageous back heel and one of his new team mates rifled in a twenty yarder which Mac reached but couldn't keep out.

Three-all at half-time, and as the whistle went, players on both sides fell to the ground, gasping for air. The game had been played at an electrifying pace.

'Nice game!' said Iain Walsh, persuading players to get up and stagger to the touchline. 'Get plenty of liquid on board, now. There's still another forty-five minutes of this to go!'

A few of the lads groaned, but most of them realised that they were in the game of their lives. They would have been happy to miss half-time altogether.

Chris didn't feel even a bit tired, even though he had been galloping all over the pitch. He pulled the midfield players and Rory into a small huddle. 'I think some of their lads are blown out,' he said. 'So I reckon we're going to get more chances in the second half. The blond lad, Bennett, he's definitely struggling. So, Rory, try to play more on the left, and keep the other backs busy. I'll run at Bennett whenever I can. Jazz, just keep me fed whenever I'm open. Stamp, you'd better drop back a bit and help out the defence.'

Walsh made a few more adjustments, trying to ensure that the defence had some more cover against Nicky's running.

It was time to go back out there.

'Listen,' said Chris as they stood up. 'Some of you know Nicky. He's come here today determined to show Iain, Sean and everyone else that the Colts should have taken him on. Most of all, he's trying to prove it to us.'

'Well, he's wrong. We don't need him. And what's more, we can do something about it. This game is ours for the taking, guys!'

The whole team went back out on to the field roaring like lions.

The second half was different to the first, although every bit as fast and every bit as exciting. After ten minutes or so, it was

176

clear that several players, mostly Gainsbury's, couldn't play at that pace any longer. They started to make mistakes, and the defence found itself under even greater pressure once the midfield players stopped running back in support. Holes appeared around the edge of the penalty box, and Chris, Jazz and Rory found themselves in more and more space.

It was only a matter of time before they scored again. As he had planned, Chris ran at Bennett over and over again, trying to pressure him into making a mistake. To his amazement, the Gainsbury defender had a bit more left in the tank than Chris had given him credit for. He stopped Chris three or four times, timing his tackles almost perfectly. It was last-gasp stuff, but it was working. Chris couldn't break through.

Eventually, though, luck was bound to desert him. Chris darted in from the right to collect a pass from Jazz, and Bennett slid in a fraction late and brought him down.

Chris found himself stretched out on the grass. It took a moment to realise he wasn't hurt, and then he rolled over. Bennett was standing over him with his arm outstretched. 'Sorry,' he said.

Chris let the bigger lad haul him up. 'You were just unluck—' he started to say, when he realised the ref was coming up and feeling in his back pocket. Chris quickly stepped between him and Bennett, a broad grin across his face.

'Hey – no need for that, ref!'

'It was a late tackle, and you had a clear run on goal,' the ref explained, with little sign of sympathy.

'He got there as soon as he could . . .' Chris replied impishly. 'And I would never have scored from there. Honestly, ref, there's no need to book him for that. You can get him later.'

The ref thought about this for a moment, then he smiled and removed his hand from his pocket. 'You don't mind having the free kick, though?' he asked.

'No, that will be fine,' laughed Chris.

The free kick was in exactly the sort of position he and Mac had been working on during the summer; three or four metres outside the box and a little to the left. The Gainsbury keeper lined up the wall to cover the near post, then took up position covering the far side of the goal.

Chris took five steps back, ran in, and dragged his foot

across the ball as he chipped it. It went just over the last player on the right-hand end of the wall, already curving. The keeper started to scramble across but the ball bent wickedly and dropped over the line barely a metre inside the near post.

Eight minutes later, Chris and Rory played a one-two on the edge of the six-yard box, and Chris smashed in his third. The whole team, having heard what Jazz had said after the first goal, ran along the touchline pretending to machine-gun people in the crowd.

'Well, that should be that,' said Rory. 'Perhaps we can take it a bit easier now.'

'I certainly hope so,' said Jazz, breathing deeply.

Chris noticed that most of the players had their hands on their hips, fighting for air. On the touchline, Iain Walsh was waving the Colts back, telling them to defend in depth for the rest of the game.

There seemed to be a few more people in the old ground as well. Sean Priest had arrived and was standing with Walsh in the dug-out. A few of the Fiorentini clan were in the stand.

Chris started playing much deeper. The next few minutes were a lot quieter. The Colts were now almost as exhausted as their opponents, and everyone seemed to be accepting the result. Well, everyone bar one.

Out on the touchline, Nicky skipped past Tollie and set off down the wing, cutting back inside once he was almost at the goal-line. He looked up, and Chris saw him frown once he realised that the rest of the Gainsbury attack was struggling to get up in support. He dragged the ball back with the sole of his boot and tried to take on Stamp, who had pulled himself back to cover. For a moment, it looked as if the Colts player had him covered, then Nicky nutmegged Stamp, swerved around him as he struggled to turn, and then raced in on goal.

Mac was forced into making a blinding save at the near post. Chris jogged back to help face the corner. The ball was cleared by the Colts' defence, but only as far as the halfway line, and then a Gainsbury player fed the ball out to Nicky again.

Chris could almost see the strength ebbing out of Tollie's legs as Nicky went at him again, swaying both ways, trying to draw the defender into an early challenge. 'He'll go out-side . . .' Chris muttered to himself, knowing that Tollie wasn't going to remember what he'd said. Before he knew what he was doing, he was running over to give Tollie some support.

Too late. Nicky faked inside and Tollie bit on it. In a flash, Nicky had transferred his weight the other way and was sprinting along the wing, leaving the defender on his backside.

Chris tried to get to Nicky, but there was too much of a gap. Nicky was already shaping up to make his cross, and this time he had plenty of targets – the tired Gainsbury attack still hadn't retreated that far after the corner. Nicky delivered a pin-point near-post centre, and the taller of the two Gainsbury strikers met it perfectly, flicking the ball into the corner.

It was the trademark Nicky-Chris goal, only this time Nicky had been setting up somebody else. Chris watched the celebrations from where he had been left stranded. As he walked slowly back towards the centre circle, Nicky ran by.

'Isn't this a game and a half?' he laughed. Chris didn't answer. 'I thought for a moment there you were coming over to mark me!' Nicky continued, beaming all over his face.

'Maybe I will,' replied Chris sourly.

There was still time left for Gainsbury to pull the game out of the fire. Chris knew the best thing he could do was get forward and win the game from up front. But Nicky had wound him up. As they lined up, Chris reshaped the Colts line-up, telling Jazz to go up front with Rory, while he lined up on the left side of midfield. He ignored Iain Walsh, who was telling him to get back into position. As the game restarted, Chris went tight on Nicky.

For the next ten minutes, Gainsbury struggled to drag one last big effort out of their tired limbs. They battered at the Colts' defence, showing lots of heart but not enough legs or skill. Chris knew that only Nicky could provide them with that extra edge they needed, and he stuck to Fiorentini like glue.

Nicky seemed to find this amusing, even when Chris got too close and sent him flying. As Chris fell back ten metres from the free kick, Nicky was grinning and clapping his hands to gee up his team mates.

He gestured to one of the others, and Chris knew he was going to take the free kick quickly. He tried to glance to his right and in that moment Nicky stabbed the ball past him and took off. The return pass was laid ahead of him down the touchline, and Nicky was running after it like a hare.

Chris, spinning as quickly as he could, set off after him. Nicky had a yard or two in hand as they pelted along the sideline after the ball. Not only was it going to be a race between the two of them, it looked even-Stevens as to whether either of them could reach the ball before it crossed the goal-line.

Chris dug deep, and stretched his long legs as he thundered in pursuit of Nicky. He could feel his heart pounding. With each stride, he took a little more out of Nicky's lead. Nicky responded and they both blazed along the line, now almost side by side. The ball was slowing; they were going to reach it. But who would get there first?

Nicky started to reach for the ball, and in that same split second, Chris committed himself into the slide, his right leg outstretched.

He hit the ground hard, eyes still fixed on the ball, praying that he had judged it right. He swung his boot across, trying to put the ball into touch, watching as Nicky swung his right foot across the ball also, trying to hit a first-time cross. There was a collective gasp from the crowd.

The impact as they hit the ball simultaneously jarred them both, and they tumbled to the ground, over and round each other. Chris looked around; he couldn't see the ball anywhere off to the side. Had Nicky beaten him?

No. The ball had jammed between them and rolled out gently behind where they fell. Chris pulled himself up and turned to collect it. Nicky, spread out on his back, could only watch as Chris turned back upfield.

People were standing and applauding. Chris felt a hundred feet tall. That tackle felt almost as good as any goal he had ever scored, and – in his heart – he knew he had proved that he was a quality player. He didn't have to play second fiddle to anyone.

He pushed upfield as quickly as he could, breathing hard, legs aching. Ahead of him, Jazz was unmarked. Any other time,

Chris could have hit the pass to him without even thinking, but he was so tired now, all he could do was run blindly with the ball at his feet. He crossed halfway, and still Jazz was in the clear. Defenders were beginning to converge on him. He could hear them closing in on him from all sides . . .

A boot snaked past his leg from nowhere. One moment he had the ball at his feet, running at speed. Next moment it was gone.

He stumbled over the tackle, and sprawled face down on the earth. He looked back, but he could tell who had taken the ball from him by the way the small band of spectators was cheering wildly.

Chris and Nicky lay on the ground, barely two metres apart. Nicky was rubbing his shin, his smile wider than ever.

'This . . . is getting . . . ridiculous . . .' he panted.

Chris tried to get up but failed. They both lay on the floor, fighting for breath.

From somewhere that sounded as if it was miles away, they heard a few ragged voices call 'Penalty!' and the ref's whistle blew sharply. Chris turned again and saw that Jazz was on the ground as well, just inside the box. He must have collected the ball after Nicky's tackle, and then Bennett had up-ended him.

Nicky crawled over to where Chris lay and clapped him on the back. 'Looks like . . . there's still work . . . to be done . . .' he chuckled. He stood, and stretched out a hand to help Chris up too. 'You still taking penalties these days, Chris?'

Chris wasn't sure he could even walk as far as the spot, never mind take the penalty, but he staggered forward anyway.

Rory already had his hands on the ball and was walking towards the spot when Chris reached him. 'I think you deserve this,' the Irish lad said, handing the ball over. Chris looked at it for a moment as if he didn't know what it was. 'Just pop it in,' said Rory, 'and we can all go home.'

Chris placed the ball on the spot and took a long, deep breath, trying to steady himself. The Gainsbury keeper looked very small in the wide goalmouth, but the goal looked a long way off in the distance. Chris realised that the sensible thing to do was to hand the responsibility back to his red-haired

fellow striker, and he was just looking round to find him when
he saw Nicky running up.

'Now what?' Chris whispered to himself. Nicky ran past and
went up to have a word with the keeper. The goalie nodded
and Nicky trotted back.

As he passed Chris, he said: 'I told him you'd go left.'

Chris almost screamed. He was so sick of Nicky's games!
Why couldn't this just be an ordinary penalty to finish off a
great game between two well-matched sides? Why had it got
to be another chapter in the running squabble between Chris
and Nicky; another 'who's better than who' contest?

Chris knew that he ought to leave the kick to Rory; he
knew he shouldn't allow Nicky to play these head games with
him. This goal could settle the game. It was important to the
team.

Chris knew all that, but lined up to take it anyway.

He teed the ball up again and took five steps back. He felt
the memory of the County Schools Cup surface in his mind,
and forced it back down. Nicky mustn't — couldn't — make
him miss again.

Two short breaths, four quick strides.

He hit the ball, and realised at once that he had hit it left.
There was a moment to fear that it would go wide, or not
wide enough; a moment to think about everything that had
happened.

Then the ball hit the back of the net, and Chris was
mobbed by his team mates. This time, they all knew, there
was no way Gainsbury could come back at them again.

182

Twenty-Four

A hot bath and about the same amount of fluid taken inside, and Chris started to feel his strength coming back. Sitting on the bench outside the dressing room, munching through a banana, Chris realised he couldn't remember a single moment of the game after the penalty.

He had never worked so hard in a game in his life. Almost every other player had said the same as they had collapsed in the dressing room, unable to move. Chris had heard spectators talking about it being the best game of youth football there had ever been, and that the TV cameras should have been at Gainsbury Town because they wouldn't have a better game on the box all season. People went up and shook Chris's hand!

It all seemed a little distant already; as if the match was a dream and Chris was just waking up. Only the warm glow of triumph remained.

It felt good. This had been about so much more than three points in the Youth League. Chris knew he had proved something today, but every player on both teams had done the same. They had all wanted to win.

He was starving, and he wanted nothing more than to get back home for Sunday dinner and a snooze in front of the Grand Prix. Most of the other Colts players were already on their way home in parents' cars. Iain and Sean were waiting for Chris, sitting in Iain's noisy old Mazda sports car.

But he couldn't leave, not yet. He had proved something today, but he had settled nothing. He had to get everything straight once and for all. It mattered even more than football.

Nicky appeared, smoothing his black hair back with his hand, blinking against the light as he stepped from the changing rooms into the autumn sunlight. He caught sight of Chris waiting, and walked over, his kit bag on his shoulder. He dumped it on the floor and sat at the other end of the bench, leaning back and sighing.

'I'm starving!' he announced.

'Me too.'

'You want to come back to our house and eat?' Nicky asked.

Chris looked round at him. Sometimes, with Nicky, you just couldn't begin to understand how anyone could be so dense.

'Did you really tell the keeper to go left?' asked Chris.

'Of course!' laughed Nicky.

'I don't always go left . . .' Chris said, suddenly unsure.

'More often than you think!' Nicky replied. 'And you always hit it left when you're tired.'

Chris had had no idea that there was any pattern to the way he took spot kicks. He had always tried to avoid doing the same thing, just in case word got around.

'So you told him to go left?'

'Yes!'

'Because of what happened at the county final?'

Now it was Nicky's turn to look confused. 'What's that got to do with it?'

'You wanted me to miss then, and I did. You wanted me to miss again today.'

'I thought we'd settled all that!' moaned Nicky.

'So did I.'

'Look, the county final was a long time ago. I promise you, I didn't want Spirebrook to lose, even though I really hated you back then. I wanted that cup as much as you did.'

'And today?'

'Today? Of course I wanted you to miss today, you dope! In case you hadn't noticed, we're on different teams!' Chris thought about that for a moment. Perhaps Nicky had a point. 'Cracking game!' Nicky said cheerfully, breaking the short silence. Chris nodded in agreement. 'Everyone told me that the Colts would murder us, but I think Gainsbury aren't a bad team . . . what do you think?'

'You looked good today,' Chris replied. The image of the

blond defender with the swollen lip slipped into his mind. 'Even that guy from Blackmoor's better than I thought he was.' Nicky giggled. Chris looked up, and found himself staring at Nicky's bruised eye. 'Who hit who first?'

Nicky ran his hand through his hair again and his laugh became a long sigh. 'Honestly. My first game with the team, and there I am, not twenty minutes before the kick off, decking one of my team mates.' Chris laughed briskly in return. He could just imagine it. 'It's all your fault,' said Nicky. 'Apparently you were supposed to meet him for a rumble in Loam Park, but you never showed. I had to stick up for you. Honestly, Chris, do you have to keep getting me into trouble?'

'I get you into trouble?!' Chris thought.

Before he could say the words out loud, Nicky continued. 'Of course, you were up in Bolton at the time, saving me from a life of crime or a good hiding from the Telford brothers. So I figured I owe you. Just like the old days, eh, Chris? You take on one of us, you'd better be prepared for both.' Nicky stuck out his hand. 'Partners, right?'

Chris hesitated. 'Nicky ... why are you playing for Gainsbury and not for the Colts?'

Nicky made a wide gesture with his hands. 'Because the Colts don't need me ... you don't need me. This lot, though, they love me! I'll soon have them eating out of my hand!'

'So ...'

'So, I'm better off playing for them than hanging around the Colts, making everyone's life a misery. It's best this way. And it's not like we won't be playing together.' Chris's face remained blank. 'Spirebrook, dummy! I'll be back there on Monday and I'll soon get Flea to give me my place back. Of course, I'll have to work on the captain, but I'm sure I can get round him too. Who is it this year?'

'Some idiot,' Chris murmured.

'That's what I heard,' Nicky said, smirking.

'It'd be good to have someone other than Jazz who can hit a pass.'

'OK, then. And this year, if you can avoid being such a prat, we'll actually win the County Cup. And the Schools League.'

'Why not the FA Cup too?'

Nicky made a face. 'Don't be stupid, Chris.' He stuck out his hand once more. 'So, team mates?'

What else was there to do? Maybe things wouldn't be the same, maybe they would. Either way, Nicky was back, and Chris was going to have to deal with that. The Colts might not need him, but Spirebrook did. And maybe, just maybe, it'd be OK to have him around.

'Team mates,' he replied, and they shook hands.

'Great,' said Nicky, standing up. 'So, can we eat now?'

'Let's go to my place,' said Chris.

'But we're having pasta! Everyone will be there!'

'Exactly,' Chris said grinning. 'Come and have some proper food. Dad's roasting this huge chicken and I'm sure he'll be happy to chuck a few more veg in the pan.'

And then he remembered a carrier bag that lay in the bottom of his wardrobe, where he had thrown it after the county final. It was ripped, almost shredded, and the contents were spilling out, but Chris knew exactly where it was.

'Besides,' he said. 'I've got a present for you. Something I was supposed to give you a long time ago . . .'